POSSESS ME

STARK EVER AFTER

J. KENNER

Praise for J. Kenner's Novels

"PERFECT for fans of *Fifty Shades of Grey* and *Bared to You*. *Release Me* is a powerful and erotic romance novel that is sure to make adult romance readers sweat, sigh and swoon." *Reading, Eating & Dreaming Blog*

"I will admit, I am in the 'I loved *Fifty Shades*' camp, but after reading *Release Me*, Mr. Grey only scratches the surface compared to Damien Stark." *Cocktails and Books Blog*

"It is not often when a book is so amazingly well-written that I find it hard to even begin to accurately describe it . . . I recommend this book to everyone who is interested in a passionate love story." *Romancebookworm's Reviews*

"The story is one that will rank up with the *Fifty Shades* and Cross Fire trilogies." *Incubus Publishing Blog*

"The plot is complex, the characters engaging, and J. Kenner's passionate writing brings it all perfectly together." *Harlequin Junkie*

A sizzling, intoxicating, sexy read!!!! J. Kenner had me devouring Wicked Dirty, the second installment of *Stark World Series* in one sitting. I loved everything about this book from the opening pages to the raw and vulnerable characters. With her sophisticated prose, Kenner created a love story that had the perfect blend of lust, passion, sexual tension, raw emotions and love. - Michelle, Four Chicks Flipping Pages

Possess Me Copyright © 2025 by Julie Kenner
Cover design by T.M. Franklin
Cover image by @GraphicCompressor (stock.adobe.com) and @SergeKa (depositphotos.com)

Digital ISBN: 978-1-958379-17-2

Print ISBN: 978-1-958379-88-2

Published by Martini & Olive Books

v-2025-1-20P

1

———————

A gentle ocean breeze ruffles my hair, and I draw a deep breath as I stand on this balcony at the Pavilion Hotel and gaze out over the stretch of the Pacific that separates Catalina Island from the California coastline. The expanse is dotted with boats, their lights twinkling like stars against the deepening twilight that's painting the water in a glow of orange and red and purple that will soon fade into an inky black.

It's breathtaking. The kind of view that can blot out the chaos of the real world, and I draw in a breath, certain that this weekend will be spectacular.

Behind me, the double doors to the Grand Ballroom are closed, but even so, I can hear laughter, clinking glasses, and the low hum of hundreds of conversations. I start to turn back to join the party, certain that Damien must be wondering where I've gotten off to, but my movement is stopped by two large hands curving against my waist.

His breath competes with the wind, and the heat of it tickles the back of my ear. My nipples tighten as a familiar electrical sensation shoots through me, awakening every cell before pooling between my legs in a sizzle of heat and longing.

I stifle a moan as his chest presses against my back, his cock hard against my rear.

A sigh of pure need escapes me, but I lift my chin and whisper, "Careful. My husband is the jealous type."

Those strong hands slide up, cupping my breasts, his thumbs teasing my nipples, hard against the fitted bodice of my slinky formal gown. "Is he?"

I try to respond but can only manage a moan as pure electricity zings from my breasts to my core. "Very jealous," I manage to whisper, barely getting the words out.

"Then he's a fool for leaving a woman as lovely as you alone for even a second."

I close my eyes. My husband, Damien Stark, is a long way from a fool.

"Still," I murmur. "If he catches us, I'll surely be punished."

His lips brush the back of my ear as he whispers. "Would you like that?" His hand slips through the slit of my skirt, sliding up to cup my sex over the thin bit of silk that makes up my tiny thong.

"Would you like me to spank you?" His voice is hot. Rough. "To take you to the edge. To lead you right to that precipice but never take you over?"

"Please," I murmur, but I don't know if I'm begging him to continue or to stop.

Continue.

The truth cuts through me, as ripe as my need. There are over a thousand people behind those unlocked doors. People who could walk out at any time, and yet all I want is for him to bend me over, push up my skirt, and take me right here, right now, with the last rays of the sun still shimmering like fire spread on the water.

"I know," he whispers. "I want it, too. But I think perhaps we should take a rain check." I whimper as he removes his hand and tidies my skirt, then turns me toward him. "Besides, we wouldn't want your husband to catch us." His dual-colored eyes twinkle with mischief. "He's the jealous type."

"He is," I say as he pulls me close, then captures my mouth in the kind of kiss that sends heat swirling through me, along with the promise of future pleasures to come. I sigh when he pulls away, still craving his touch but knowing that it will have to wait.

"You're a tease," I say, letting myself bask in the glow of this enticing game and this gorgeous man. His raven-black hair with just a dab of gray at his temples. That sculpted jaw, with a roguish hint of stubble. And those eyes—one amber, the other black—that mark him as someone exceptional.

He holds out his hand. "I think it's time we join the party, Mrs. Stark."

"Anything you say, Mr. Stark."

I step toward the doors, then change my mind and tug him to a stop. "Have I told you today how much I love you?"

"You tell me with every glance. With every touch. With every kiss." He strokes my hair, hanging in loose waves around my face. "And your love is a miracle I never thought I could deserve. And I never tire of hearing the words."

"In that case," I say, "I love you."

He cups my cheek, his expression as tender as I've ever seen it. "I love you, too, Nikki Fairchild."

I lift my chin. "Nikki Fairchild Stark, thank you very much."

"And thank god for that."

We share a smile before he tugs open the door, and we trade the last remnants of twilight for the hum of opulence that fills the huge ballroom. The subtle glow of crystal chandeliers. The tuxedo-clad waitstaff moving through the room with trays of crystal flutes bubbling with champagne. The string quartet tucked into a corner and playing a soft, elegant arrangement.

The Pavilion Hotel is a spectacular venue, and its Grand Ballroom is the pièce de résistance. Marble floors gleam beneath the sparkling chandelier. Lush arrangements of white roses spill from silver vases. And the aroma of delectable appetizers dances on the air.

The murmur of conversation fills the room, punctuated by bursts of laughter or the occasional pop of a champagne cork. It's the same vibe as opening night at the theater, and everywhere I look, I see glitz and glam. Not surprising since the cheapest ticket to this charity event cost five thousand dollars, allowing only entrance to the party and a chance to bid in the auction. The most expensive ticket priced out at a cool hundred thousand, and the five purchasers at that level are in the running to win a spa weekend for two in Manhattan. Not that extravagant considering the ticket price, but as Matthew Holt, the organizer and sponsor, pointed out, the goal is to raise money for the charity. Not to spend it.

Personally, I'm hoping Damien or I win. We could easily afford a weekend of pampering, but the idea of "free" pampering seems so much more fun. Possibly because even after so many years as a billionaire's wife, I still have sticker shock at so many of the things that are part of the Damien Stark lifestyle.

Mostly, I'm just glad to see how much money the ticket sales have raised. Sixty percent of the proceeds are going to the primary cause—the conservation and restoration of a huge catalog of films from Hollywood's Golden Age. Twenty percent is going to fund classes and programs to help lower-income teens learn both basic life skills and skills that could lead to a job in the entertainment industry.

The final twenty percent will fund the creation of a charity that helps out-of-work actors and other film and television professionals in need of medical or housing assistance.

The theme, of course, was chosen by Matthew, a man I sometimes think of as the entertainment industry version of Damien. And who, at the moment, is across the room, greeting guests and shaking hands in a sea of stunning gowns and sharp tuxedos.

Behind him, scenes from various Vivien Lorainne movies play on screens set up throughout the ballroom. This event is all about that classic film star who was taken far too early in a violent death at her husband's hands.

The murder shocked the Hollywood community so many years ago, as did Carlton Lorainne's subsequent suicide in jail a few weeks later. Over and over, he'd claimed his innocence, fueling a Hollywood mystery that's been debated for years. As far as the public knew, the couple was deeply in love. But as one biographer pointed out, murder is often a crime of passion. If Carlton believed Vivien was cheating on him...

As a fan, I've wondered about the truth for most of my life. But I also know that it's impossible to ever know for sure.

"Penny for your thoughts," Damien says, and I realize that I've stopped in the middle of the ballroom, my attention drawn to one of the many screens that line the walls, this one playing newsreel footage of her death.

"Just thinking about how sad it is," I admit. "She was such a talent."

"She was," he says, then kisses my forehead. "Did you know she used to work in a soup kitchen? Even after she became a star, she would go every Saturday to help out. I think she would like knowing that the funds from this auction will do good."

I smile, then squeeze his hand, forcing my melancholy aside so I can simply enjoy seeing the memorabilia and, perhaps, choose something to bid on myself.

We start across the room, where a cluster of posed mannequins shows off original costumes from her films, and display tables let the guests get a closer look at the queen's crown and the assassin's knife from one of her most beloved thrillers. It's impossible not to feel the weight of history in the room, as if every artifact and image carries the essence of a bygone era.

"Nikki. Damien." Matthew smiles as he catches up to us, taking my hand and raising it for an elegant kiss. "I'm so glad you were able to come."

I've known Matthew for a while now, and he reminds me a bit of Damien. Devilish good looks and the kind of presence that commands a room. A form of gravitas that comes from not only being in control, but knowing that you deserve to be.

"We wouldn't have missed it," Damien says. "It's an excellent cause."

"Will you be bidding on anything?" he asks with a glance toward me.

"I'm sure we will, though I don't know what. We're still working our way toward the auction tables."

"Well, even if you don't find something you want, feel

free to bid the price up," Matthew winks. "It's all for a good cause."

Damien chuckles. "We'll take that under advisement. In fact, we'll go take a look right now."

We congratulate him again on the spectacular event he's put together, then continue toward the cases filled with the items that will be up for auction within the hour.

When we're just a few feet from the first case, Damien tugs me to one side. "Did you notice?" he whispers.

I shake my head, not sure what he means.

"So many eyes on you as we crossed the room." His voice, low and full of heat, is as enticing as a caress. "Women who want to be you. Men who want to own you. To touch your skin. To kiss your breasts. To cup your ass in their palms. To slide a hand through the slit in your skirt and explore your heat. To feel your desire."

"Damien…" My cheeks are burning, both with the fear that someone might overhear and in response to his words. A hard, visceral response that makes me want to blow off the auction and hurry upstairs to our suite. "Hush."

But he only steps closer, one hand at my waist as he leans in, his breath on my ear as he says, "But I'm the one who'll have you in my bed tonight. Only me. Say it, Nikki."

"Only you," I whisper. I turn my head, leaning back enough so that I can meet his eyes. "It's only ever been you."

The smile that touches the corners of his mouth is so full of heat and joy that it takes my breath away. Even with three kids and so many years behind us, he can still make my heart flutter the way it did when I first saw him, this man who is the love I never expected and never thought I deserved.

"Thank you," I whisper, then kiss his cheek.

He cocks his head, his eyes narrowing just a bit. "For what?"

"For our life. For loving me."

"We gave each other our lives," he says. "And as for loving you...." He trails off with a soft chuckle. "I'm not sure I had a choice about that."

"I know," I say, understanding what he means with perfect clarity. Because that's how I feel, too.

He lifts my palm to his lips and kisses it. Then he cocks his head, and I see a hint of amusement flash across his face. "We probably should make a better effort to see the displays before the auction starts," he teases. "Then let's track down Sylvia and Jackson," he adds, referring to his brother and sister-in-law. "They probably think we ran off."

I glance around, not seeing either of them. "Or they did." I grin. "Syl was telling me they haven't had a night away from the kids in over a month. They had the look of a couple with something other than an auction on their mind."

"I think I'm jealous," he says as he presses a hand to my back, leading me toward the displays.

"Don't get any ideas, Mr. Stark. I'm not missing out on the chance to bid on something of Vivien Lorainne's." As Damien well knows, she's my favorite classic actor, and her last movie and only musical—*The Red Carousel*—has been one of my favorite films since childhood.

"Maybe I should just buy the entire collection and call it a day."

I turn to look at him, afraid that he's serious, then relax when I see his face.

He chuckles.

"Don't laugh," I say. "You know perfectly well that could have been a legitimate threat." For that matter, I'm certain the only reason he doesn't buy out the entirety of the items up for auction—is that it would steal the fun from other potential bidders. Plus, he's determined to win the bid on at least a few items for me. And I'm certain he's looking forward to the back-and-forth of bidding against someone else with the means to purchase and the wherewithal to bid against a man like Damien Stark.

I stop at the first case, drawn to a glittering silver and turquoise snake bracelet. I recognize it from *The Red Carousel* right away. It had been a gift to the heroine from the dead lover she mourned—and who came to her in dreams when she wore the bracelet. Vivien herself had found the bracelet during her travels overseas and had suggested it for the prop in the film. Now, here it sits, coiled on a velvet cushion. It's stunning—delicate yet bold, with tiny emeralds gleaming in the eyes of the snake.

I want to call over one of the attendants to open the case and let me try it on, but the "Display Only/Not For Sale" placard stops me.

"It suits you," Damien says, his voice low.

"It's fabulous." I turn to frown up at him. "I love the idea of an auction—especially one with memorabilia from all of her films— but including something that can't be bought … well, that just doesn't seem sporting."

He taps my lips as if trying to erase my frown. "It's probably earmarked for the traveling collection," he says, referring to the props, costumes, and other memorabilia that will travel the globe, visiting various museums and institutions as part of the effort to raise funds for the charity. "We'll find something else wonderful for you to bid on."

I'm still disappointed, but he's right. Sometimes, all the money in the world can't buy what you want. I suppose that's a good lesson to remember. Especially considering that after so many years with Damien, it's not an issue that I bump up against often.

Nearby, a cluster of people *oooh* and *ahhh* over another case displaying a sequined gown she wore in a dark drama in which the naive young woman became ensnared in the clutches of a man determined to take her money and her innocence. Another case holds an ornate feathered head-piece and, further down, an embroidered silk robe from an iconic bedroom scene.

"You would look lovely in that," Damien says.

"I have more lingerie than I need," I tell him. "Especially since my husband never seems to let me wear it for a full night. Or a full hour," I quip.

He comes closer, lowering his voice to a whisper as he says, "Your husband must have a keen eye to know that what's hidden is even more beautiful than the garment that hides it."

"If you're trying to seduce me," I tell him, "you're doing a very good job."

"Are you saying I have to seduce my wife?"

"Wouldn't want you to get complacent, Mr. Stark." I toss a smile and a wink over my shoulder before I move on to the next case, this one with various items from her home.

"I wonder what's inside it," Damien muses as I linger over a leather-bound journal with only the letters VL stamped on the cover. It's small, the kind of notebook you'd tuck into a purse or leave by your bedside for late-night thoughts.

"I'd love to find out," I admit." I can almost see her, pen in hand, pouring her secrets onto the page, and I'm over-come with an urge to bid on this journal. I imagine the feel of the leather in my hand, the rasp of a pen nub against the paper. And I think of all the secrets it holds.

"I can call over an attendant," Damien says with a knowing smile. "Open the case. Let you take a closer look."

Yes, yes!

The words ring through my mind, but I can't make them come out. Instead, I shake my head, wondering at my reaction.

"Nikki?" Damien studies my face with a frown.

"I'm fine. Lightheaded." It's not a lie. I've eaten too little and drunk too much. "It's probably a fascinating read, though," I say as I point to the description: *Private Journal, Vivien Lorainne. November 3, 1945 through January 12, 1946.*

I shoot a glance toward Damien. "This was the journal she kept when she was filming Carousel and also when she moved back here after the film wrapped. It ends the day before she was murdered."

I shiver, on one hand, not wanting to touch something that feels tainted by the way she was so brutally beaten just one day after she'd completed this journal. But on the other hand, wanting to get into her head. To read in her own words what was going on in those last days.

The truth is, I've already read some of the entries in this journal. One of her biographers quoted from journal entries in *The Tragedy of Vivien Lorainne*, an unauthorized biography that was published a few years ago. But to now have the opportunity to read all of her thoughts, and not just those the biographer chose ... well that seems like an opportunity I can't pass up.

"You want it," Damien says.

"Is that morbid?"

He shakes his head. "She's your favorite actress. You've read, what, all of her biographies?"

I nod.

"That's not morbid. It's curiosity. And caring."

I want to tell him that I feel like the journal is supposed to be mine. That once I have it, I'll be able to find answers. More, that I'm *supposed* to find answers. As if it's up to me to finally tell the world what happened to Vivien. What secrets she hid. And why her husband snapped and killed her, beating and stabbing her. If, in fact, it was him who did it.

She'd managed to run from the house, but escape did her no good. She was found dead on the nearby beach early the next morning. Carlton, her husband, was raving when the police arrived, begging them to believe that he didn't kill her. That the murderer was someone named Basil.

But neighbors testified that there was never any guest named Basil at the cottage, and the police were unable to find any evidence that such a man existed. On top of that, neighbors reported that the couple had recently been having frequent, violent fights.

In the face of all of that, the police determined that the crime was a murder ... quickly followed by Clayton's suicide while in custody. A suicide that convinced the police that Clayton was guilty and that he'd killed himself out of guilt and shame.

But there were others who knew the couple from when they'd lived in Beverly Hills, and every one of them swore that Vivien and Carlton were devoted to each other, that they'd never been violent with each other, and that Basil must have been a real person who burst in to destroy their lives, then slipped away, never to be heard from again.

No concrete answer was ever found. More, some now say that anything surrounding her has been cursed.

"She was a kind and talented woman who cared about her work and the industry," Damien says when I tell him as much. "If I believed in curses, I'd say that hers has long faded. And the circumstances of her death certainly expanded her name recognition. Her films are all excellent, but there's no denying that the murder is one of the reasons she's still in the public eye after all these years. Did the mysterious Basil kill her?" he adds in an announcer-style voice. "Did her husband? Did they work together? And if so, why?"

I shake my head, grinning a little at his showmanship. The truth is, I have no idea. But my eyes go to the journal.

I know it's silly, but I can't shake the feeling that the journal is somehow calling to me. As if it wants me to have it. As if all the answers are hidden in those pages.

Which, of course, is ridiculous since the journal has been reviewed by several biographers.

Still....

With a shrug, I tell Damien that I'm going to bid on it. Hell, maybe it *is* calling to me. Maybe Vivien wants me to have it. Maybe my fascination with all things Vivien Lorainne makes my purchase inevitable.

Maybe I just need retail therapy.

"Go right ahead, baby," he says, the words and his tone making clear that I can bid as much as necessary to ensure that the journal is mine.

2

———————

Two hours later, I'm the proud owner of the small, leather-bound journal into which Vivien Lorainne once poured out her secrets. That simple fact makes me giddy, and I can't wait to dig in and lose myself in the story hidden within those pages.

Sadly, I don't yet have it in my hands. The auction's policy is for each guest to pick up their items as they leave the gala, presumably so as to not interrupt the festivities, and also to prevent the confusion and headache if someone sets an item down and then can't find it again.

I understand the rule, but now that I've won it, I want to hold it. I know I'm just excited by having placed the high bid, but I can't shake the feeling that once the journal is in my hand, I'll understand my Hollywood idol so much better. Maybe I'll even learn all of her secrets.

And maybe—just maybe—I'll find a clue as to why she was murdered ... and by whom.

"Nikki!"

I turn to see Sylvia—Damien's former assistant and now sister-in-law—waving as she navigates through the crowd, her silver gown complementing her short, dark hair and giving her a polished, regal look.

"I was beginning to think I wouldn't see you until the brunch tomorrow," she says, pulling me into a hug. "I'm dying for a look at that journal."

"Me, too," I admit. "I'm tempted to tell Damien it's time to go, just so I can get my hands on it."

"Well, he's talking to Jackson." She nods across the room. "So I'm in the same boat you are."

I laugh. "Except not literally." While Damien and I have a suite at the Pavilion, Jackson and Syl are actually staying the night on *The Veronica*, the yacht on which he lived when he first moved to Los Angeles.

"We decided to do a long weekend with the kids," she'd told me a few days ago during one of our frequent late-night calls. "They think the boat is cooler than a hotel suite."

"Is Ronnie in charge right now?" I ask, referring to their eldest daughter.

"I'd trust her," she says. "That kid's been the most responsible one in the family since the day I met her. But, no. I conned my brother into the job. After brunch tomorrow, we're going to do a family adventure and explore the island. By both land and sea." She shrugs. "Then we'll head back to the mainland around sunset."

"Why not just stay another night?"

"Jackson's got a meeting about a project in Dubai."

I nod, not the least bit surprised. As one of the world's most sought-after architects, he works with clients from all over the globe.

A waiter passes with custom cocktails, and we each take one that is pink and fruity, then sip it as we continue to talk, catching up on gossip about our friends—Jamie and Ryan are smitten with baby Maia, Jane and Dallas are pregnant again, Matthew Holt is still single, and will probably stay that way, and on and on and on.

We're deep into planning a girls' night when I see a familiar face. A lanky blond man with piercing eyes and a slightly crooked smile that is currently aimed at me.

"What?" Syl asks as I lift my hand in response to his wave.

"Help me out," I say as the guy approaches. "I can't recall his name."

"Nikki!" the Mystery Man says, easing up beside me and brushing his fingertips down my arm.

Syl's brows lift, but she extends her hand. "I'm Sylvia. Nikki's sister-in-law. And you are...?"

"Greg Keeler," he says, and right then, I could kiss Sylvia.

"I'm so sorry, Greg," I say. "I should have jumped right in to introduce you two. Greg was almost a client," I tell Sylvia. "He decided to go on to bigger and better things."

Greg chuckles, then slides his arm around my shoulder in a casual, we're-all-buds-here manner. I give Sylvia *the look*, and she takes a step in the opposite direction—clearly hoping Greg will follow—as she says, "Okay, spill. Because that sounds like a story."

Greg stays planted firmly at my side as he explains that he'd come to me about doing some custom software for his startup. But he abandoned the startup when he was offered an excellent position at a well-established company.

"Bigger and better things," I quip, twisting for my purse and, in the process, shaking free of him. I'd mostly forgotten Greg, but now I recall with great detail the wash of relief that had flowed through me when he'd told me we wouldn't be working together.

He's a nice enough guy. But the man is a toucher. Not just me. Everything and anything. It got to the point where I would move anything I didn't want fiddled with from my office before we had a meeting.

Unfortunately, at the moment, his constantly busy hands and fingers have targeted me, and I sigh with relief when I see Damien and Jackson across the ballroom.

I lift a hand, urging them to join us. By the time they do, Greg's made his goodbyes and taken his busy fingers toward the display cases. Where, I'm sure, he'll drive the staff crazy by trailing his fingertips on the glass and asking for an item to be taken out of the case—and toyed with.

"Who was that?" Damien asks, and all thoughts of Greg's busy fingers go out of my head as Damien's arms go around my waist.

"Greg Keeler," I say. "I know him from work."

"Hmm," Damien says in a tone I know quite well.

"Stop it," I say, laughter in my voice. "He's not remotely interested in me.

"The view I had suggests otherwise."

I hear the humor in his voice and tilt my head back. "Jealous, Mr. Stark?"

"Always," he teases. He knows as well as I do that jealousy is pointless. For me, there's only Damien, for now and for always.

His arms tighten around me, and a sensual buzz cuts through me along with the unspoken message—*you're mine.*

As I revel in Damien's touch, Jackson steps in behind Sylvia, his hands resting on her shoulders as she leans against him.

Like Damien, Jackson has dark hair, a striking jawline, and a way of standing and walking that conveys both confidence and power. They're friends now, as well as brothers, but the early months after Damien learned of Jackson's existence were tough on all of us. Thankfully, that's all in the past. Now, Damien and Jackson and Syl and all of our kids make up the core of the close-knit family I'd always wanted, but never believed I would have.

"They're shutting things down," Damien says, opening his jacket so I can see the plastic-wrapped journal tucked safely into an interior pocket. "Shall we grab a drink in the lobby?"

"They're going to say no," I say, with a nod toward Jackson. "Kids waiting on the boat."

"The kids should be asleep on the boat by now," Jackson says, moving to Sylvia's side and hooking her arm through his. "I think a nightcap sounds great. We can make plans for a longer get-together when we're all back home."

"Perfect," Damien says. He brushes a kiss over my forehead. "And after that, Mrs. Stark, I have a surprise for you."

～

"You sure you're okay to walk?" Damien asks as we stand with Syl and Jackson—all of us now slightly tipsy—in the Pavilion's ornate lobby to say our goodbyes.

"I'm fine," I assure him.

"It's not far," he promises.

"This is why women wear heels and have the babies," Syl says, shooting a grin in my direction. "At the heart of it all, they're the ones who are wimps."

Jackson chuckles, and he and Damien share a look. "Sounds fair," Damien says with a shrug.

"Very astute assessment," Jackson agrees, making Syl and I break into a fit of giggles that probably has more to do with the cocktails we drank than the actual humor of our banter. We've just managed to control ourselves when someone across the lobby calls out, "Mrs. Steele!"

I turn in that direction as Sylvia waves. "Dr. Hart! I didn't know you were here."

Dr. Hart turns out to be Dr. Franklin Hart, who Sylvia introduces to us as a Los Angeles-based psychologist. "And an occultist," Damien adds. "It's good to see you again, Franklin."

I look between the three of them. Dr. Hart doesn't look at all like a man who cavorts with ghosts. Sylvia and I have had Tarot readings for fun, but I didn't think she was into the occult. And while Damien is fascinated by everything, I doubt he's been using a paranormal consultant to help build Stark International. Which boils down to my question: "How on earth do you all know each other?"

"Sophia," Damien says flatly, referring to the woman who had almost been a sister to him—and had once tried to kill me. "She had regular sessions with Dr. Hart for a few years," he says.

I only nod. I've forgiven Sophia a lot, but as far as I'm concerned, the sessions never did her much good.

As for Syl, she explains that they met through her lifetime bestie, Cass, who has a bit of a woo streak. "She dragged me to a lecture—sorry, Dr. Hart, but it's true. I was all prepared to be bored and unconvinced." She grins. "But it was fascinating."

"We'll have to come to one of your lectures," I say, glancing at Damien, who doesn't look convinced but smiles politely.

"I'd love to hear your impressions," he says, and Sylvia adds that she'll send me the info to sign up for Dr. Hart's newsletter.

"Were you at the auction?" Damien asks.

"I was. In fact, I bid against you on that journal."

I stand up a little straighter. "I thought your voice was familiar. I couldn't see who else was bidding."

"Why would you want the journal?" Syl asks, voicing what would have been my next question. "Is there something odd about it?"

"I'm a collector of Hollywood memorabilia," he says. "But to be honest ... well, yes. The journal holds a special interest for me because of its connection to her house."

I nod. "You mean the rumors that her house here on the island is haunted."

"Indeed," Dr. Hart says. "If she wrote that journal while in a haunted house, some of that energy might have been absorbed."

"Oh." I glance toward Damien, feeling suddenly as if the journal inside his jacket is emitting protoplasmic waves. Or whatever kind of a vibe haunted things give off.

Damien squeezes my hand, stepping closer. "You actually believe that house is haunted?"

"It does have that reputation."

"I think gossip and tourism are the more likely source of those rumors. She was beaten almost to death in that house, and we know she'd had many arguments inside it with her husband. Surely, it's that drama that fueled the haunted house stories. That and the vacation company that owned it for the last few decades pushing the Haunted Hollywood narrative."

Dr. Hart grins. "Just because they pushed it doesn't mean it's not true."

I can't help but agree with Dr. Hart, but Damien just shakes his head. "At any rate," he says, "it was a pleasure meeting you. Are you staying on the island for a while?"

Dr. Hart nods. "Since I was here for the auction, I

thought I'd stay for a few days of relaxation. I have a room here at the Pavilion."

"Enjoy that," Damien says.

"We'll be here for a few days as well," I tell him. "Maybe we can have coffee one morning. I'd love to hear some of your ghost stories."

He chuckles. "They're not all ghosts, but I'd be happy to share. And yes, you can reach me here."

"Us, too," I say, though when I look at Damien's face, I wish I'd kept quiet. I can't quite read it, but I'm afraid I may have just interfered with his plans for a romantic weekend in our suite.

But if that's the case, I'm sure Dr. Hart will understand if we wait on coffee until we're back in Los Angeles.

We promise to touch base, then part ways, with Dr. Hart passing Damien his card before he steps back into the hotel. I watch as Syl and Jackson head toward the pier. As they fade from sight, Damien starts to walk in the same direction along Crescent Avenue. I tilt my head. "You have plans, Mr. Stark?"

He shrugs, looking almost boyish. "Just hoping to take an evening stroll with my wife."

"In that case, Mr. Stark," I say as I hook my arm through his, "lead the way."

We walk in silence for a bit, enjoying the night and the simple pleasure of each other's company. After a few blocks, he nods toward my feet. "You're really okay walking in those?"

"I'm fine for now," I say. "And while I'm enjoying this," I say, then add a tinge of heat in my voice, "I should confess that I was looking forward to going back to our room." I smile up at him. "This walk is probably great for my thighs and ass, but I had a different kind of workout in mind."

"Did you?" His voice is low and a little growly in a way that has my body responding in all sorts of wonderful ways. And makes me all the more frustrated that we're still going in the wrong direction.

"As far as I'm concerned," he says, "your thighs and ass are already perfect." He stops, then faces me, reaching around to squeeze the ass in question. "Yup. Perfect."

"What are you up to, Mr. Stark?" I ask as our walk continues—in the wrong direction. I'm pretty sure I already know—the beach. Where else could we be going? And while I'm very fond of my dress, I'm more than willing to sacrifice its hem to a walk in the surf with Damien.

But just as I'm certain we'll be veering off to the water, he turns in the opposite direction and starts leading me up a hill. That's when I have to admit, if only to myself, that I haven't a clue what my enigmatic husband has in mind.

Still, I'm not worried. Damien never fails to please. Because even if he does make a misstep, he makes up for it in the most delicious of ways.

I defer to the hilly terrain and take off my shoes with their impractical heels.

"You're okay on the pavement?"

"This late? It's cool enough." I dance forward a bit, enjoying the way my skirt brushes my thighs, not sure if I'm buzzed on champagne or Damien.

Damien. Definitely Damien.

We've been married for over a decade and have three kids. And yet, I still feel like a girl in my twenties falling desperately, helplessly in love.

"Hey," I say, taking his hand and tilting my face for a kiss.

"Hey, yourself," he whispers, his soft kiss so full of heat that I want to melt right then.

We hold hands as he leads me into a neighborhood.

"Have you checked in with Evelyn?" I ask, in a complete non-sequitur.

"I have," he says. "The kids are having a grand time with Gran and Gramps."

"Evelyn insists she hates that," I say, fighting a laugh.

Damien shakes his head. "I think she loves it." Evelyn Dodge has been a fixture in Damien's life since childhood when she acted as his agent during his years as a professional tennis player, both as a kid and as an adult. She's been my friend and pseudo-mom for years, and a huge improvement on the woman who biologically has that title.

And since she's now married to my father, I can legitimately call her Mom. And my kids call her Gran. Damien's right, of course. Brassy and bold, Evelyn will go to her grave pretending that she's still too young to be "Grandma," thank you very much. While all the time, she's giddy inside.

I've seen the look in her eye.

I glance up to tell Damien all of that, and only then do I notice a street sign.

Metropole Avenue.

"You brought me to Metropole?" I pause to look at him, my mind whirring. "Are we heading to Hollywood House?"

I can't keep the eager note out of my voice. *Hollywood House* is what the vacation rental company that bought Vivien Lorainne's house after her death named the property. And, of course, they listed it in the *Haunted Mansions* subsection of their catalog.

At less than two thousand square feet, the house isn't actually a mansion. From the pictures I've seen and the things I've read, it's a cute little blue cottage with white trim. It has a covered porch, a huge back patio with a view of the ocean, three bedrooms, a living room, and a dining room. The cottage was Vivien's favorite place in the world, and she lived there permanently, leaving it only when she was filming or traveling.

"If we're staying overnight, I wish you'd told me," I say, my secretly aching feet no longer aching. "We could have brought our luggage."

"I'm not giving away anything," he says. "Besides, I think I'm insulted that you don't trust me to have taken care of that."

"You make a good point, Mr. Stark."

He chuckles as we round a bend. "Eyes on the pavement, okay?"

"I already figured it out," I say, but he simply stares me down.

"Fine," I agree, far too giddy to argue. I let him guide me the rest of the distance, then draw in a breath when he moves behind me, his hands on my shoulders. "We're here."

It's exactly as I've seen it in photographs. Only one thing is different—there's a For Sale sign in the yard. And hanging from it is a smaller sign, bright red with white letters: SOLD.

3

***

S*old?*

I glance toward the sign, lit in the warm glow of a street lamp, then back at Damien, his face alight with humor and just a hint of something else. Nerves, I think. Except Damien very rarely gets nervous.

"You?" I say, my voice little more than a whisper. "Damien, did you buy Vivien Lorainne's house?"

He spreads his hands in a *little boy and the cookie jar* gesture.

"For me?"

"For us," he says, moving in front of me and putting his hands on my hips. "Good surprise, bad surprise, or weird surprise?"

My laugh seems to echo from this hill all the way down to the beach as I throw my arms around his neck. "Good," I say. "And also a little weird. But in the best possible way," I add, rising on my toes to kiss him as his hands slide to cup my ass. The kiss is long and deep and fully worthy of a gift of the two-thousand-square-foot variety. And when I pull away, I'm as giddy as if I'd just downed a bottle of champagne.

"You're sure? You're not worried about the rumors? Hauntings and all that?"

I wave a hand, brushing away the words. "Vivien Lorainne's house." I shrug. As far as I'm concerned, that's all that needs to be said.

A white picket fence surrounds the house, and when he opens the gate, I practically skip through and onto the front porch. When he joins me, I grin. "I'll say this for you, Mr. Stark—there's never a dull moment."

"And there never will be."

We share a smile as I lean against the porch railing and study this man who not only still loves me, but still surprises me, managing to make every one of our days together just a teensy bit better than the one before.

Luckiest girl ever, I think, and I can't help but wonder what I did to deserve Damien in my life.

He dangles the key with a knowing grin. "You want to do the honors?"

I definitely do, and I hurry to snatch the key from his hand, then shoot him a sideways glance. "You do realize we already own a cottage on an island?"

"Ah, but it's a different island. And that one's actually *on* the beach. This is on a hill with a *view* of the beach."

I fight a laugh. "You do know how to split hairs."

"And this is historical," he adds. "Totally different." He gives me an exaggerated shrug. "But if you don't want it…"

He plucks the key from me. I laugh and dance toward him, easily taking it back because we're both laughing too hard to put any real effort into the game.

Once it's safely back in my hand, I put my fist over my heart. "I would say I can't believe you'd do something like this for me, but I know that you would. Thank you." I slide the key into the lock and start to turn it.

"*Nikki.*"

I look over my shoulder, something in his voice sending a shiver through me.

"Are you sure?"

I frown. "I just told you I was. What's wrong?"

He shakes his head. "I don't know." He sounds almost confused, and Damien is never confused. "I just—I just thought I should tell you that you don't have to accept it."

"Damien?"

"I left an escape clause in the contract," he says. "If you don't want it, we can just void the purchase."

"An escape clause?" That's not the way Damien usually operates. I know that he'll always give *me* an out. If I didn't want the house, he'd just turn it into a rental or hold on until the market improves and take a profit. But voiding the sale entirely…?

"Why?"

He shakes his head, something in his expression making him look almost as confused as I feel. "Just felt like a good idea. But you want it? You're sure?"

I nod, realizing as I do that he's taken the journal out of the inner pocket of his tux … and out of its plastic bag. He's shifting it from hand to hand, and for a moment, I want to snap that it's humid and to put that thing away before it's damaged.

But I bite back the words. "It's Vivien Lorainne's house. You knew I'd want it, and you were right. You still are." I grin. "I think Dr. Hart spooked you."

He chuckles. "You know, maybe he did."

I meant the words as an explanation for Damien's out-of-character reaction, but now I can't help but think about the darkness that this house has seen. This is where Vivien lived with the man who killed her. The man who bashed her over the head and stabbed her, leaving her to escape to the beach and die alone.

He denied it until the day he, too, died. Over and over, he cried out from jail that he wasn't the killer. That it was someone obsessed with Vivien. Someone dark and evil named Basil who had insinuated himself into their lives.

But, of course, neither the police nor historians ever found such a man.

Is this a house I truly want to enter?

I hesitate, fully intending to turn back to Damien. To tell him that maybe this isn't such a great idea. But I don't. Instead—almost as if someone is urging me forward—I put the key in the lock and push open the door.

A chill rushes up my spine as I step over the threshold into the pitch-black entryway, with Damien right behind me, his hand on the small of my back.

And as the door closes behind us, I think I hear, beneath the creak of the hinges, a woman's voice whispering

—*Nichole! Nichole! What have you done?*

4

———

"Did you hear that?" I ask, stopping just over the threshold so that Damien has to walk around me.

He cocks his head, frowning slightly. "Hear what?"

"A second ago." I hug myself, fighting a chill. "As I came in. I thought—" I cut off my words, realizing I have no idea what I was going to say. That I'd heard my name? That I'd felt an odd sense of being watched?

I shake my head, feeling more than a little silly. "Never mind. Ignore me." I smile up at him. "I think my husband let me drink a little too much this evening."

The corner of his mouth twitches. "That's a shame because your husband asked the realtor to leave a bottle of Champagne on ice. But I suppose he can drink it all by himself."

I fight my own grin as I slide into his arms, realizing that the strange sensations that had set my skin to tingling are now only a memory. "I can probably handle one glass," I whisper. "Besides, we have to toast the house. Champagne is almost a requirement. Champagne and sex," I add, reaching up to tug one end of his bowtie, unraveling it in a single, smooth motion before deftly undoing the first two buttons at his collar.

"I do love the way you think." He brushes a kiss over my lips before stepping away with a promise that he'll be right back. I feel his absence keenly—strangely—like a sharp stab of loss coupled with fear. I'm about to call out for him, but then his shadow slides into the room, followed immediately by the man himself with a bottle of champagne and two empty flutes.

"Nikki?" He puts the bottle and glasses on a sideboard and then hurries toward me. "You look like you've seen a ghost."

I laugh, the sound tinny to my ears. "Maybe I am a little spooked." I shrug. "The house does have a history, after all."

He brushes his fingertips down my bare arm. "Everything has a history. And I think you and I know better than anyone that your past doesn't have to taint your present."

I close my eyes as he pulls me toward him, and my arms go tight around him, this man who knows me so well. Who knows the demons from my past that still haunt me.

Demons he helped me fight, even while fighting his own.

We've survived so much, and we built something wonderful.

This house will be wonderful, too.

I draw in a breath as I step back, then smile up at him. "I think we need to explore. And drink a toast in every room."

"Mrs. Stark," he says, his voice teasing. "Are you intending to get me drunk and take advantage of me?"

I flutter my lashes. "I guess you are as smart as everyone says."

He laughs, then pours us each a flute of bubbly. We toast

the living area where we're standing, a cozy space anchored by a stone fireplace and softened with worn wood floors and high, beamed ceilings.

I turn in a slow circle, taking it all in. The built-in shelves that line the walls. A vintage loveseat positioned near a coffee table. A wide picture window, beyond which the surf shimmers in the moonlight. I smile, feeling strangely at home in this unfamiliar place.

Damien takes my free hand and leads me into the charming kitchen. A vintage dining set sits in the nook by the bay window, and I imagine lazy mornings with coffee and the ocean as our backdrop. A hallway leads to the bedrooms, including a spacious master with a set of French doors that open onto a private patio.

Every room is in perfect order—dust-free and tidy, just as a vacation rental should be. But this is no typical vacation rental. Because mixed in with the generic trappings that ensure a traveler's comfort, there's also Hollywood memorabilia scattered throughout. Framed photos from Vivien's most famous films line the hallway, and a small glass case in the corner of the den houses props from her movies—a sequined clutch, a feathered hat, a delicate tiara. It's like walking through a time capsule, each piece a connection to a history that's always fascinated me.

Still, despite the Hollywood decorations and the strange trill of sensation that had spooked me as I entered, the place feels almost generic. As if it could be the cover photo for a vacation rental catalog.

Honestly, I'm almost disappointed.

Not that I'd wanted to move into a haunted house, but I'd let myself believe that this cottage was somehow the connection between Vivien Lorainne and myself. Instead, it just feels like a house that contains a few photos and props.

And yet....

I can't deny that something about this place feels familiar. And not. Like stepping into a memory that doesn't belong to you. Which, of course, makes no sense whatsoever.

"Well?" Damien's hand presses lightly on the small of my back as we return to the living area.

"It's incredible," I tell him, and despite that little knot of disappointment, I mean the words completely. "But you have to stop buying me presents every time you turn around. Especially such extravagant ones. People will think you're spoiling me."

"People would be right." He takes my hand and leads me to the sofa. "So are you saying I shouldn't give you the one present I still have left?"

I cross my arms as I shift on the cushion to face him better. "Um, excuse me? The journal is already mine. Hand it over." I hold out my hand, palm up, and he reaches into his interior pocket for the small journal, then puts it in my palm so that the embossed initials — *VL*—are facing up.

But there's something else, too. Whereas before, I'd only noticed Vivien's initials, now I'm looking at those initials surrounded by an ouroboros.

"I don't remember the snake being on the cover," I say to Damien. "Do you?"

He frowns at the journal as I scowl at the design of a snake eating his tail. Unlike the embossed initials, this has been burned into the leather. Like a brand.

Damien's brow furrows. "Honestly, I can't remember one way or the other."

"I can," I say. "It was just the—"

"What?"

I shake my head, suddenly realizing that I'm uncertain. I

was excited to see Vivien's initials. As for the design surrounding them, maybe my mind just ignored that.

"It must have been there," Damien says. "It's not as if someone would have branded the journal between the time we bid and the time we picked it up."

"Right," I say. "We just didn't notice."

Our eyes meet, and I can't help but wonder. But Damien only shrugs as if he's not concerned at all. And if he's not, why on earth should I be?

"It looks good this way," I say as I move my finger around and around. Tracing. Following. "Yes," I say as if I've just made an important decision. "I like it."

Damien takes the journal, surprising me by tracing the outline of the snake himself. "It's almost as if it knew," he murmurs, his voice barely audible.

"It? Knew what?" I have no idea what he's talking about.

His smile is slow as he passes the journal back to me, then slips his hand into his pocket again, this time pulling out a velvet jewelry box about three inches square.

I look from the journal to the box to Damien. "You really are spoiling me. What on earth do you have there?"

"Why don't you open it and find out?"

I take the box, the velvet smooth against my fingers, then lift the hinged lid. Inside, nestled against black satin, is Vivien Lorainne's snake bracelet. The one listed as "Display Only." The one I'd admired and mourned as unavailable.

"Damien," I whisper. Tears prick my eyes as I carefully lift it out of the box. The silver coils gleam in the dim light, each curve impossibly intricate. Tiny emeralds glint in the snake's eyes while turquoise stones dot the band, their color deep and mesmerizing. "Damien, this is…"

I trail off, unable to find the words. "But it wasn't for sale. How—?"

He only shrugs, his eyes gleaming with satisfaction. "You wanted it."

"Thank you." My throat is clogged with tears as I slip it onto my wrist. The silver is cool against my skin, and the weight of it seems strangely comforting. "I don't even know what to say."

He takes my hand, then brushes a kiss across my knuckles. "You don't have to say a thing. It suits you."

I glance down at the bracelet again, watching the way it catches the light. For a moment, it almost seems to shift, the emerald eyes gleaming like they're alive.

I tilt my head, studying my husband. "You said all our luggage is here?"

"All unpacked by elves."

I grin. "In that case, Mr. Stark. I think you should wait here. As they say in the movies, I'm going to go slip into something a little more comfortable."

"Oh, really?" He settles in, his arms spread on the back of the sofa, looking relaxed and powerful and so sexy I consider just forgetting about the silky 1940s-style negligee I'd bought for our night after the auction.

But no...I want to seduce my husband properly. "Have another glass of champagne," I suggest, picking up my flute before heading toward the master bedroom. "And remember—anticipation is half the fun."

"It is, Mrs. Stark," he says, his voice so full of heat it's almost a caress.

I resist the renewed urge to forget the damn negligee, then hurry to the bedroom.

I find the garment hanging in a chifforobe, and I quickly strip, then slide it on, enjoying the feel of the satin over my bare skin. I'd found the negligee in a consignment shop, and since it's from the forties, I'd had to buy it for this trip. Now

I'm glad I did. It's ankle-length, with thin straps and a low-cut bodice. Sexy as hell, and yet somehow demure, especially when paired with the matching—albeit sheer—robe.

For a moment, the memory of that strange voice when I'd opened the door comes back to me. The voice. The snake branded onto the journal. It must mean something, but—

I shake my head, having lost my train of thought. Apparently cocktails and Champagne aren't a good combination if I can't even hold a thought in my head for a moment.

I run my palms over the negligee, enjoying the sensual feel of the material under my hands. And what do thoughts matter, anyway, when soon enough Damien's kisses will send all thoughts scurrying, leaving nothing but hot, delicious need.

With a happy sigh, I do a quick turn in front of the free-standing mirror in the corner of the room. It's a period piece as well, its gilded frame curling into intricate flourishes at the edges.

I turn away from my reflection, then look back over my shoulder in what I hope is a seductive pose.

And then I freeze.

It's gone in an instant, but for a moment—the briefest of moments—it wasn't me reflected in that mirror.

It was Vivien—blood trailing down her forehead, her eyes wide with terror, and her mouth open in a silent scream.

5

"Nikki?"

I spin toward Damien's voice, catching a glimpse of him in the doorway before I suddenly find myself in his arms, my face pressed against his chest as I try to control my breathing.

"Baby, what is it? I heard you cry out."

I shake my head, my eyes squeezed shut, certain I couldn't have seen what I thought I'd seen.

"Sweetheart, talk to me." His voice is soft, but I hear the edge of fear, and I draw a breath, then lean back, still safe in the circle of his arms.

"It's nothing," I tell him. "Just my imagination. Too much to drink. Too much talk about haunted houses." I lift my wrist and glance at the snake bracelet, feeling silly and more than a little embarrassed. "Too much Vivien and thoughts of murder."

I pull back, shrugging as if it's nothing. Nothing at all.

Because, I tell myself, it *is* nothing.

"All right," Damien says in the voice he uses when he's trying to get a straight answer from one of our kids. "It was just your mind playing tricks. But what exactly did your mind do?"

I shake my head. "Forget it. Truly. I just—active imagination, okay? I—I thought I saw something."

"Yes, but what?" He tilts my chin up so that I have no choice but to look at him. That, or close my eyes. And I know he won't stand for the latter. His hair's a little mussed, the tux jacket is now missing, and a few more buttons on his shirt are open, revealing a smattering of chest hair.

The sight calms me. *Normal*, I think. *Just me and Damien. And everything is normal.*

I really hope that's true.

"Nikki?"

I look up, realizing I still haven't answered him. "Vivien," I say, my voice small. I turn my head just enough to glance at the mirror and then back at him. "In the mirror. Her head was bleeding. The way he killed her, hit her. The way they found her on the beach."

"Oh, baby." I don't even feel the shift, but suddenly, I'm completely in his embrace, his head bent as he murmurs soothing words. How I'm tired. How it's been an emotional day. And how, yes, perhaps the stream of alcohol throughout the day and into the night wasn't the most sanguine of plans.

I know he's right. Add in the fact that we enjoyed our suite at the Pavilion last night so much that I'm now operating on very little sleep ... and, well, it makes perfect sense that I'd be half in a Vivien Lorainne-induced dream state.

And yet...

His eyes narrow. "I know that look. Tell me."

"It's just silliness. I'm fine, really."

He waits, his eyes never leaving my face.

"Okay, okay," I say, as if he'd been haranguing me. "I just

—I know it sounds silly, but I swear I saw her. And I think—well, I think she wanted to tell me something."

For a moment, he just looks at me. Then he reaches out to stroke my cheek and tuck a strand of hair behind my ear. "Is that really what you think?"

I know his voice, and he's not humoring me. He's truly asking if I think the rumors are true—if this place is haunted. And if, perhaps, the ghost of my favorite star is reaching out to me.

It's as if he's flipped a switch inside me. As if the fact that he takes what I believe at face value makes the whole world clearer. As if his trust—his love—is the mirror I can hold up to see reality.

"I—no," I say, as a stray tear streams down my face. "But I really did see her in the mirror. Even if it was only my imagination."

"I'm not surprised," he says gently. "We've been talking about her all day. Thinking about her movies. Her murder. And now we're in her house—something you weren't expecting. I'm sorry," he adds, his voice taking on a somber tone.

I gape at him, shaking my head. "No. Damien, no. This house—it's the most wonderful gift."

"But maybe it was too much to toss onto a day already full of the history of Vivien Lorainne?"

"No." I take both of his hands in mine. "I love this house. And the timing was perfect. I mean, hello? When else would you give a gift of Vivien's house if not after a gala that's all about her?"

His smile is gentle. "But?"

"There is no *but*," I tell him honestly. "It's just that—you make me feel special every day. Every single day. Little things. Big things. Silly things. But this...."

I trail off as I pull my hands free of his, then start to walk the room, as if I'll find the right words hidden in a corner.

"Too much?"

I laugh. "From the average husband, yes. From you, no. On the contrary. I think that's what makes it special. It's a huge gift. It's a freaking house. And one that I'm sure cost more because of its history. But the only thing that mattered to you was that it matters to me. That it's a piece of Hollywood history—of Vivien Lorainne's history—and so you bought it. And maybe any man with your means would have done the same, but I don't think so. It's just another piece of the puzzle, and I love it."

"The puzzle?"

"All the ways you show that you love me," I say. "Except I'm wrong. It's not a puzzle. It's a patchwork quilt, and with everything you add, you make me feel that much more loved and that much safer."

"I'm glad," he says, then tilts his head, flashing a mischievous smile. "So a potentially haunted house makes you feel safe?"

I smirk. "Okay, that's fair. But I don't think she was in the mirror to hurt me. I think maybe she was welcoming me to her home. And, you know, just forgot to do her hair and make-up before sending me the message."

We share a smile.

"I think your imagination is on overdrive, baby. But in case I'm wrong, I can think of one way to break any spell that might be lingering in this house."

I lift my brows. "You surprise me, Mr. Stark. I didn't realize you were so well-versed in the occult. Or is that how you made your billions? A bit of nightshade and eye of newt?"

"I don't know about that," he says. "But I'm pretty sure there's one thing that always conquers dark magic."

"And what's that?" I ask, my pulse quickening as he moves closer.

"Love." He's right in front of me now, his hands sliding the robe off my shoulder to pool on the ground, leaving me in the silky, white nightgown.

"And it doesn't hurt that you look like an angel," he whispers. "Though I plan on tarnishing your wings soon enough."

"Oh, really?" My voice is a tease and a challenge, and I can see by the gleam in his eye that he's accepted it.

"I have to," he says, his face deadpan and serious.

"Have to what, exactly?"

His arm slides around my waist, and he draws me closer to whisper in my ear. "I have to make love to you, Nikki. I have to tease you. To touch you. Stroke you. I have to brush my fingertips over every inch of your body, searching out all of your most sensitive places."

"Oh." It's the only word I can manage.

"My fingers first," he says, his voice so hot it's like living flame. "Then I have to taste you. Your lips. Your nipples. Your cunt. I want you hot for me, baby. I want you to melt. I'll take you higher and deeper than we've ever gone. Wilder. Hotter. Faster. Love and heat and passion and longing. Friendship, respect, and pure, burning need. All of it, Nikki. Everything we are to each other, we'll pour it out into this bed, into this house. We'll mark this house as ours. And we'll kick anything dark that thinks it resides here right back to the hell it came from."

I'm breathing so hard, I can't manage a reply. Not in words, anyway. My body is screaming *yes*. Begging, *please*.

Crying out for him to take me before I burst from the primal need that is filling my every cell.

His clever fingers pull the nightgown over my head so that now I'm standing naked in front of him. He gives me a devilish look, then brushes his fingertip over my lips before trailing it down my neck, between my breasts, then between my legs to tease my clit.

I moan, already wet and desperate for a bolder touch. But that hand stays put—both torment and tease—as he uses his other hand to tilt my chin up so that I have no choice but to meet his eyes.

"Fuck the demons," he says. "This house is ours."

6

———————

This house is ours.

The word seems to hang in the air as his mouth claims mine, the fingers of one hand twined in my hair as the other cups my bare ass, pulling me tight against him.

Need and heat surround us, writhing like a living thing determined to drag me down even while riling me up. To steal my breath and shatter my composure.

Damien.

This man who shatters me with every kiss. Whose touch makes me feel desperate and vulnerable.

And, most of all, loved.

I need that tonight, here in this strange place. I need him to anchor me, because otherwise I think I might lose myself in the walls of this house.

I don't know how. I don't know why. I only know that something dark is nipping at me. At us.

And I can't fight the dark without Damien.

"Damien." His name is a plea. A demand.

A prayer.

I'm not even sure what I want other than everything. His fingers inside me. His mouth on my lips, my skin, my sex.

Him.

I want him. I need him.

I want to kneel at the altar that is Damien.

And he damn well knows it.

"Damien," I say again. "Please."

His fingers barely stroke my clit, but it's enough to steal thought and feed need until that's all I am. Need and want and lust—but for Damien. Only for Damien.

His fingertips brush my cheek, so soft that I moan in protest because I'm craving hard, jonesing for wild. Needing what only Damien can offer.

And when his mouth covers mine—not softly, but with a hard, violent passion that sets my soul on fire— I moan into the kiss, my body pressing against his, my fingers clutching at his shirt. There's never a time when I don't want Damien, but right now it's more than want. It's need. Hell, it's survival.

Something in this house is pulling at me. I don't understand it. I can barely even think about it with my head so full of lust and heat. All I know is that if I don't lose myself in Damien, I will lose myself completely. He's my husband, my best friend, my mate.

He's my savior. And tonight, I need him to take me all the way to heaven.

"Open your eyes," he says, the words so soft, yet undeniably a command.

I comply, only to realize that he's turned us so that we're facing the mirror. Me, naked. My body flush, my lips swollen, and my nipples hard. He's standing behind me now, his hands on my hips, his head bent so that his lips are near my ear.

"Touch yourself," he whispers as his hands slide up my body to cup my breasts, his thumbs teasing my oh-so sensitive nipples.

"Damien." His name is barely a whisper.

His lips brush my ears as his eyes meet mine in the mirror. "Disobeying, Ms. Fairchild?"

I don't answer. Not in words, anyway. But I do as he ordered, sliding my hand between my legs, feeling my own slick heat even as I feel the hard press of his cock—still in his tux—against my bare ass.

I stroke my clit, my eyes locked on Damien's in the mirror as that sweet excitement builds. As my legs seem too shaky to support me. As my core goes hot and slick with need. I'm close, so close, but I don't want the explosion. Not like this.

With a gasp, I close my eyes, leaning back against him. He's so hard, and all I want is for him to tug down the damn zipper and take me right now, hard and fast and with all the heat and danger and wildness that seems to haunt this house.

"Please," I beg, because now that the thought has entered my head, I know that's what we have to do. What the house needs us to do. "Damien," I beg as the fingers of one hand twist my nipple before he forces me to my knees, then bends me over the side of the bed, the ornate bedspread rough against my bare skin.

I hear the metallic zip as he frees his cock, then the pressure of his body as he bends over me, his rock-hard cock teasing my ass as he trails kisses down my spine before ordering me to prop myself up on my elbows. I do, and he takes my breasts, his hands engulfing them, not in a gentle caress but hard and wild. An anchor. A port in a storm of wild passion.

So he can find his way back.

The words fill my head even as Damien thrusts inside me—hard and fast, so that my body grates against the spread as if he's marking me with each thrust. It's wild and raw, and though I cry out for him to move slower, all he does is tighten the grip on the back of my neck so that I'm locked in place. *His.*

His hard, raw groan rocks through me when he comes, and for a moment, he lays on top of me, breathing hard. Then I feel his body tense, and with a curse, he's up and off the bed. "Nikki," he says, my name sounding heavy on his lips. "God, Nikki—I'm sorry."

I sit up, not even thinking as I grab one of the pillows to cover me, when never once have I felt the need to be modest around Damien.

He drags his fingers through his hair. "I don't know why —I didn't mean—*Fuck.*" Then he's standing in front of me, one finger gently lifting my chin. "I didn't mean to use you like that."

I meet his eyes. "I'm yours," I say simply. "Whatever you need, Damien. You know that."

He does know that—because that's who we are to each other. It's how we've always been. It's the reason we found each other, and he knows that.

And I think the fact that he's not saying that scares me more than any voice in a doorway or ghost in a mirror.

"Damien?"

"Maybe we should head back to the Pavilion. Order some champagne up to the room. Shame to let the penthouse go to waste."

I think that's a fabulous idea. But when I open my mouth, what comes out is, "*No.*"

He only looks at me, then nods. "The house." He brushes my cheek. "We'll make it ours."

He pulls me close and kisses me again, long and deep and tasting like Damien. And this time, when we make love, it's long and languorous and gently sweet.

After, I lay in the circle of his arms, wondering if I should tell him the truth—that I wanted hard. That I wanted wild. That I wanted—needed—to be used tonight. That I am craving a darkness wrapped in love. That I need the pain. Not the tip of a blade to my flesh, but his hand on my ass, his cock relentless. My wrists bound.

I need it tonight.

Except I'm not sure it's me who needs it. Maybe it's Vivien, I think, as I curl into Damien's heat.

No, I think, as sleep tugs me under. *It's the ghosts.*

I shiver. We have to figure out how to get rid of them. Because ghosts don't simply vanish. Not in a place like this. And certainly not without a fight.

oonlight streams through the window as I wake slowly, my body feeling gloriously achy, and his name on my lips ... *Carlton.*

Carlton?

With a gasp, I sit bolt upright as I come fully awake, the remnants of a sensual dream that didn't star Damien lingering like dust in an abandoned house—there, but impossible to truly see, much less catch.

For a moment, I stay completely still, the soft whisper of Damien's steady breathing grounding me.

I tell myself it was only a dream. The stories about Vivien's murder. The strangeness of this house. The bracelet and the journal. All of that meshing together as my mind weaves a spiderweb of tales. Me, Vivien. Damien, Carlton. But it's not real. It's only my mind playing tricks. Nothing more than dreams and imagination.

I lay back down, my body pressed against Damien's as I close my eyes and try to slide back into sleep. But the words keep me awake. Soft words like whispers. A dream, I think, wondering if sleep has finally come for me. But the whisper is far away, and my body goes tense as I try to listen. As I try to make out the words that are just beyond the edge of hearing, curling through the dark like an insidious secret.

I tell myself it's not a voice. Just the sounds of the night. The wind. An owl. The house settling or a breeze ruffling the leaves of nearby trees.

But I know it's something else. Something worse.

Something terrifying.

I hesitate, taking a moment to make up my mind. I know I should stay beside Damien. I know I should ignore it—whatever it is—because most likely it's my mind playing tricks.

But even knowing that, I can't ignore the lure of the whispers, and I slip out from under the covers, doing my best not to disturb Damien.

My bare feet meet the cool wood floor, and I shiver. The air feels colder than before, almost damp, and the sensation of being watched prickles at the back of my neck. I glance back at Damien, wondering if he's awake, but he's still lost in his dreams.

I slip on the sheer robe, then ease out of the bedroom, closing the door behind me and wincing at the creak of the hinges. The hallway stretches before me, and shadows dance in the light thrown by the wall sconces.

I move slowly, the uneven creaks of the floorboards beneath my feet marking each tentative step. I'm not sure where I'm going or why. I only know that I need to keep moving forward toward some unknown goal.

When I reach the living room, I let out a small sigh of relief. I'm not sure what I was expecting, but seeing the furniture in its familiar layout seems to ground me. At the same time, though, something feels off. As if the room has been holding its breath, waiting for something.

Perhaps even waiting for me.

I tighten the belt of the robe, fully intending to turn around and go back to bed. Instead, I settle into the armchair, then pull the soft, knitted blanket onto my lap. Vivien's journal sits beside me on an end table, and I pick it up, the leather shockingly warm in the cold room. The weight of it surprises me, too—it's heavier than it looks, as though it carries more than mere words within its pages.

Wistfully, I trace my fingertip over the snake imprint, still wondering why I hadn't noticed it back at the hotel.

Not that it matters. All that matters is what's on the pages.

I need to see what's on the pages.

The words fill my head, yet I have the strangest sensation that they aren't my words at all.

I push the disturbing thought down. This is Vivien Lorainne's journal. The actual book she wrote in with her own hand. Perhaps she even sat in this very chair as she wrote. And now I have the chance to read her words. To get in her head. To come as close as possible to actually being my Hollywood idol.

I shiver, telling myself it's from anticipation, not fear. And then I take one deep breath and start to open the book.

Except I can't. The journal sits in my lap, my hand on the cover, but something is holding me back. I'd been so excited to win it, to own a piece of Vivien Lorainne's life, but I can't deny the cold fingers of dread that seem to creep up my spine.

I tell myself I'm being silly, then flip the journal open before I can talk myself out of it. The pages are yellowed with age, and I catch the faintest scent of old paper. The ink is faded but legible, and Vivien's script, though small and curly—is readable.

I start at the beginning with Vivien's thoughts about the post-war world and how the film industry was booming. She was excited by several projects, and was even starting her own production company.

I smile as I read, fascinated by not only her thoughts on her career and the world, but on the little things she included, such as the menu for the Thanksgiving dinner she held that year, and the guest list, which is a Who's Who of Hollywood and politics.

Mostly, I'm enjoying reading entries on the routine of her life, such as the very first entry:

November 3, 1945

Spent the day at home, as Carlton insists I rest. He says filming Carousel drained me, and I suppose he's right. The part was exhausting, and I keep replaying the final scene, wondering if my performance was enough. Carlton, of course, says I was perfect. And what I so love about him is that he truly believes that.

I can't help but smile, loving how such simple words humanize the silver-screen goddess I've idolized for years.

Eager for more, I flip through the pages, skimming the entries even though I know I'm going to go back and read every word from the beginning. I'm about a month in when I see an entry that stops me cold.

December 4, 1945

Carlton's restlessness is becoming trying. In so many ways he is still the tender, sweet man I fell in love with. And yet he's been harsh lately in a way I can't quite define. I fear that he is jealous, as he's mentioned Basil again. I have no memory of the man, but Carlton insists that he made an appearance at the garden party last month, and that he has been lingering around the studio. I suppose he could be a fan, though it is frustrating that Carlton insists that I must have seen him, and when I deny knowing even what the man looks like, he fumes, clearly not believing me.

I'd like to say that Carlton's jealousy is endearing, but it is not. On the contrary, it is exhausting, and I fear that his jealousy of a man I've never seen and certainly don't love will be the thing that shatters us.

I frown, wondering about this mysterious Basil. That Carlton was jealous of him isn't news. That obsession was documented in every Vivien Lorainne biography I've read. But though I know that several of her biographers were given access to this journal—and included many quotes from it—I've never seen that particular entry before. For that matter, I've never seen an entry in which Vivien mentioned Basil at all. Which, considering the mystery surrounding the mysterious Basil, seems very odd.

That oddity only multiplies as I get further into the journal—and find more entries about Basil. About Carlton swearing Basil was present at all sorts of events ... and Vivien worrying about Carlton since she has no evidence the man even exists.

And with every Basil sighting, it seems as if Vivien and Carlton draw further apart.

December 8, 1945

Once again, I didn't see the man that Carlton swears was watching me. I told him to stop mentioning Basil. That I have no interest. That the man is nothing to me. I was so frustrated the words flew out of me, and Carlton flinched as if they were blows.

And then—oh, dear god—he lashed out. He caught himself,
but for a moment, I truly believed he was going to hit me.
What happened to the man I loved?
More important, what happened to the man who loved me?

My chest tightens, and I flip ahead, desperate to know what happened. But the next entry I find is weeks later, and nothing but mundane words about a shopping trip full of charming observations and thoughts about the perfect present for her friends and for Carlton.

I flip forward, finding more mundane entries—dinner parties, gossip from the set, notes on a new perfume.

I have my finger on December 12, the last entry I fully read about a costume fitting, and I'm about to close the journal when movement on the page catches my eye. I glance down instinctively, because surely any movement was a shadow cast by the moonlight.

But no.

Dear god, the print has changed.

My body goes cold as that realization runs through me. The words I'd just read are gone. Changed. Altered.

How?

I have no idea. All I know is that they've been replaced by a new entry with the same date. And while part of me wants to hurl the journal across the room, I can't do it. I have to see. I have to know.

I'm both curious and compelled. And, yes, I tilt my head to the page, and I read.

December 12, 1945

It's not Carlton I'm afraid of anymore.
I woke to the sound of whispers. Soft, but insistent. They

*were coming from the hall, but when I opened the door, there
was nothing there.*

*The bracelet was missing this morning. Carlton says Basil
took it. I don't believe him, but I can't find it anywhere.*

Am I imagining things? Or is he?

I'm starting to forget what's real.

I shiver, the journal seeming cold in my hands.

And I can't help but wonder—am I starting to lose my
grasp on what is real, too?

8

———

Damien and I walk in silence down the path that leads from the cottage to the beach. The sound of our footsteps marks our progress, and the distant music of the ocean lapping onto the beach is leading us to our goal.

"Are you going to tell me?"

Damien's words are soft, full of genuine concern.

"Tell you what?" I ask, even though I know exactly what he's talking about.

"You've been quiet all morning. Are you feeling okay?"

"Sure. I'm fine." My stomach twists at the lie. But how can I tell him the truth? What I saw in the journal last night. The whispers I heard once I'd slid into bed. The scent of an unfamiliar perfume that hung heavy in the air, raw and cloying?

There's something wrong with me.

And I can't tell Damien. I can't say a word.

You can. You have to.

I push the small voice down, telling myself I just need a

little more time. I need to figure a few things out. Once I have answers, that's when I can talk to Damien.

The fingers of my right hand stroke the snake bracelet I'm wearing on my left wrist, the motion calming me. I tense when Damien takes my hand, breaking that connection.

"What?" The word is sharp, almost a snap.

His brow furrows. "I'm worried about you. You don't seem fine."

Get it together. Get it together for him.

I draw a breath, then tilt my head and offer him my best smile. "It's nothing. Really. Just...weird dreams." I start to tell him about the December 12 journal entry. About how it changed after I read it. About Basil and what I think he did to Vivien. About what maybe he's doing—

No.

I shake my head, trying to clear the wild thoughts as the bracelet grows warm around my wrist. I'm just tired. That's all. Strange stories and not enough sleep. A terrible combination.

Damien takes my elbow and tugs me to a stop, his eyes searching mine. "Your dreams. How are they weird?"

I shrug. "Honestly, I don't even remember. I just didn't sleep well."

"No," he says. "You definitely didn't."

I frown, more in response to his concerned tone than his actual words. "What are you talking about?"

"You were sleepwalking last night. Do you remember?"

"I—what? No, I wasn't."

"No?" He looks almost amused.

"I've never walked in my sleep. Not ever."

"That you know of."

"I was awake when I got out of bed, Damien. I couldn't sleep, so I went into the living room."

"Maybe so," he says. "I was asleep when you left the bed. But I saw you come back. I spoke to you. You just slipped into bed, said something about cooking, then rolled on your side and started snoring."

I bristle, not sure if I'm more annoyed by the allegation of sleepwalking or of snoring.

"What did you do in the living room?"

I frown. "I just read a little." I don't mention that I was reading the journal.

"What exactly did you read right before you came back to bed?"

"I—" I cut myself off, toying with the snake bracelet as I try to remember. I'd read the mundane journal entry about the costume fittings. But then it had changed. Then the entry was about Basil.

And try as I might, I don't remember getting back into bed beside Damien.

Relief floods through me. I'm not crazy.

I laugh out loud. I'm not crazy, and the journal isn't possessed.

I was dreaming. Of course, I was dreaming. That's why the words on the page changed—because they only changed in my dream.

I rise onto my tiptoes and kiss his cheek. "Apparently, your wife sleepwalks."

He cups my cheek. "Apparently, she does."

"It's probably because of the house. Unfamiliar. The bogeyman. All that jazz." I slide his hand from my cheek to my lips, then kiss his palm. "But I have you to look out for me."

"Always," he says, the word so full of love I feel tears prick my eyes.

"We should get going." I nod to indicate that we've

stopped on the path. "I'm kind of starving. Those late-night walks work up an appetite."

He laughs, the worry fading a bit from his face. And when it does, something inside me cries out. Screaming that he's wrong to be soothed. That we both are. Because everything is off—is wrong.

But the words won't come. Instead, I hear a little mantra in my mind—*it will be fine, it will be fine, it will be fine.* And so I force my worries back, then twine my fingers with his as we hurry the rest of the way to the beach and the dock where *The Veronica* is moored.

Sylvia spots us right away, rising from her seat at the pretty picnic table on the beach. "I was beginning to think you got lost."

"We're three minutes late," Damien says, glancing at his watch.

"The great Damien Stark? I thought he was never late for an appointment." She grins as she hurries toward us, then hugs us both in turn.

"Where's Jackson?" I don't have to ask about the kids—I can easily see Ronnie and Jeffery playing in the surf.

"In the galley." She nods toward the boat. "Playing chef."

Damien chuckles. "That's something I want to see," he says, then kisses my forehead before heading toward the boat.

I take a seat across from Sylvia, who's already half into a mimosa. She pours one for me, and I take a sip, relishing the bubbles and, frankly, looking forward to getting buzzed. Maybe even drunk.

Anything to forget.

Sylvia props her elbows on the table and rests her chin in her hands as she leans forward to study me. "Okay, tell. What's wrong?"

I take a long swallow, downing the mimosa. "It's just...weird stuff at the house."

"Oh! So it is haunted!" She leans forward. "Creaky floorboards? Flickering lights? Full-on poltergeist? Tell me everything."

Despite myself, I laugh. "Nothing so dramatic. Just—it's hard to explain. Weird vibes," I say, realizing as I speak that I feel more like myself now. Was it all my imagination last night?

"A house with a vibe. That doesn't sound too bad."

"Yeah, well, I also thought I saw something in the mirror last night."

"Something?"

I pick up the pitcher and refill my mimosa, then take another long swallow. "Vivien."

Her brows shoot up. "Wait. What?"

"She was bleeding." I stifle a shiver. "It was ... well, it really freaked me out."

"Hell, yeah, it did." She lowers her voice. "What did Damien say?"

I shift my gaze to the boat, then back to Syl. "I don't think he believes me."

Saying that out loud is a relief. More than that, I think it explains the weird tightness growing inside me since yesterday. An irritated itchiness. A sense of something not being right.

And no matter what he may think, Damien's not making it better for me. Anger bubbles up, cold and hard. He's not making it better at all. Not the way he's supposed to. Instead, he's just humoring me. And what the hell does he—

"Nik?"

I jump, then glance around, getting my bearings. The beach. The boat. The picnic table.

"Sorry. Mind wandering." But I don't meet Syl's eyes. Instead, I look into my flute so she won't see the confusion in mine. Because for a moment, I wasn't here. I was back in the house. I was standing in that living room. And I was making plans to get what I need from Damien.

To get what I deserve.

The thought spins unanchored in my head, and I stand up, then pace behind my chair, idly stroking the snake bracelet.

"You're freaking me out."

"It's not me," I say, forcing the words out. "It's the house."

"You truly think it's haunted?"

The words seem to hang on the wind.

Yes, I want to say. *Yes, dammit, and help me.* I want to tell her about my fears. About the journal and Vivien and Basil. But I only laugh and shake my head. "No, of course not. It's just…" I trail off, then shrug. "It's just a good story."

Sylvia doesn't laugh. Instead, she leans back, her expression thoughtful. "What if you're wrong?"

I bristle. But I also lean in, intrigued by both her words and her tone. "How do you mean?"

She shrugs, looking more than a little uncomfortable. "It's just … I don't know. But, well, if any house is going to hold onto something, it's that one. The fame. The violence. It's like you walked into a Blumhouse script."

I'd lifted my mimosa, but now I put it down without taking a sip. "So you really do think it's haunted?" Something unpleasant spins in my gut. That half-sick feeling you get when a secret is accidentally spilled.

"I'm just saying that houses carry energy. And Vivien's life—and death—had plenty of it."

I glance toward the beach. I hadn't seen Damien leave the boat, but he's with the kids now, helping them build a sandcastle. Their laughter dances on the wind, and I can't help but smile.

I turn to Syl, realizing I know exactly what to say. "It's just my imagination," I tell her. "Don't let my goofiness make you paranoid."

She rolls her eyes. "Well, of course, it's not really haunted. You're probably just feeling a little weird since it used to be your favorite star's home."

"And she was murdered there," I add, as fingers of ice seem to tickle my spine. "It's not haunted..."

"But maybe a little tainted?"

"Yeah. Maybe that's it." But that's not it. Because how can I tell her that I feel more than just history in that house?

I should tell her.

I should tell Damien.

I should tell someone.

But the little voice inside me says no. The voice that I think came with me from the house.

"Come fill your plates!" Jackson's voice booms out from the boat, and I glance toward the water, where Damien waves in acknowledgment before racing his nephew to the boat while Ronnie looks on and laughs.

I start to stand, but Sylvia grabs my hand across the table, keeping me down. "Let them go first," she says. "I want —well, it's probably silly, but I want to give you something. Or, well, lend it to you, anyway. At least while we're on the island."

"Um, okay." I have no idea what she's talking about.

She reaches up, then fiddles with something behind her neck. For the first time, I notice the delicate silver chain upon which I assume a pendant is hanging, now hidden beneath her tank top. She pulls the chain free, revealing a small, silver crucifix that I recognize immediately.

"How on earth did you get that?" It was Vivien Lorraine's crucifix, and Syl had bid on it at the auction, but lost.

Syl casts a sideways glance toward the boat. "Jackson wanted to surprise me with something I wanted, but since it was an auction, he decided to hire someone to bid on whatever I bid on."

I laugh. "In other words, he paid way more than he needed to."

Delight dances in her eyes. "He said it was worth it to surprise me. That, and all the money's going to a good cause."

"Well, that's true. But—wait a second," I say, recoiling as she extends the necklace to me. "What are you doing?"

"It's not from a movie," she says. "It was Vivien's when she was a little girl. The story is that her mother gave it to her on her deathbed and told Vivien it would protect her. She lost it not long after she moved to Catalina—or she thought she did. It was found in Carlton's safe deposit box after his death."

I frown. "He took it from her?"

"I don't know. But everyone says she wore it every day after her mother died until they moved here." Her eyes meet mine. "Until she moved into that house."

The house didn't want it. The house made Carlton take it away.

I push back, shocked by the force of the words in my head.

"Nik?"

I shake my head, fighting the urge to recoil from the thing. "I can't take that. Jackson got it for you."

"Just a loan. Just while you're on the island." She meets my eyes. "Please. I can't explain it. I just—I just really want you to wear it."

I want to wear it, too, but somehow I can't seem to reach for it.

And that makes me want it all the more.

"Nik?"

"I—" I'm fighting for the words. Wanting the necklace. Hating the necklace.

Needing the necklace.

"I have a terrible time with those kinds of catches." I swallow, then meet her eyes. "Can you put it on me?"

She studies me for a moment, then nods. "Sure." I watch her walk around the table, a sense of dread building. Fear that she won't be able to manage. Fear that she'll drop it. That it will somehow end up in the surf, washed away, never to be found.

But then her fingers touch my neck, and I feel the cool metal on my skin, then the weight of the pendant as it tugs the chain down once she's fastened it.

Vivien's crucifix. Her totem. Her protection.

Relief washes. Over me. *It's mine now.*

But some small voice inside my head only laughs, and tells me that it's come too late to do any good at all.

9

———

Damien holds my hand as we walk the path back to the cottage, neither of us speaking. It's a comfortable silence, and at the same time, it feels charged, sparking with things left unsaid, like the air before a storm.

A storm, I think, then shiver.

The storm has yet to come.

"Are you cold?"

I shake my head. The ocean air is cool, but even in short sleeves, I feel pleasantly warm. Like a winter fire is burning in my belly and spreading through my veins.

He pauses as we reach the back door, but he's the first to speak. "You've been quiet."

I smile up at him. "Just basking in the day." It's not a lie—brunch had been delightful. Talking with Syl and Jackson. Watching the kids in the surf.

But it's not the whole truth, either.

Ever since we left the boat, a strange unease has been curling in my stomach. It's not the food or the champagne. It's something intangible, something I can't quite put my finger on. I brush the feeling aside, chalking it up to over-thinking. After all, this is supposed to be a weekend of relaxation and romance.

Stepping inside the house seems to ground me. We've barely spent any time here, and yet the creak of the floorboards seems so familiar. So welcoming.

As we enter, I look around this house that I already love. That already feels like mine. As if we've been coming here for years and years.

I reach for Damien, then sigh in relief when his hand immediately closes around mine. I look up, expecting a smile, but instead, I see darkness. Shadows on his face. A tightness in his jaw.

A shiver runs through me—*that's not Damien!*—and I yank my hand free as I turn my head away, my gaze moving to the long shadows cast by the sun sneaking past the gaps in the curtains.

"Nikki?"

I hesitate, but when I turn my head to look at him, he's Damien again. On the outside ... and on the inside, too.

Relief washes through me, so powerful it makes me lightheaded.

"Baby, are you okay?"

I've bent over, my hands on my knees. Now, I straighten slowly, then put my fingers to my temples and shake my head. "Too many mimosas and too much sun, I guess."

He moves closer, and I bask in the tenderness when he puts one hand on my hip, then strokes my hair with the other. "You should sit."

"No. I just—I'm going to go change. Will you just get me a big glass of water and maybe a few ibuprofen?"

His gaze roams over me, as if he's searching for secrets, but he nods, then turns toward the kitchen as I hurry into the bedroom, desperate to change into snuggly leggings and a tee. *He's Damien. He is, he is, he is.*

I head first to the bathroom, then lean close to the mirror. "And you're Nikki," I whisper, meeting my own eyes, terrified that those words seem so strange.

I focus on the crucifix pendant. "Please," I whisper. "What's wrong with me?"

But instead of an answer, I feel a darkness well up inside me.

Rip it off. Just reach up and rip the damn neckless off.

The urge is right there, so potent I can feel it in my fingertips, but I don't understand it. It's a beautiful pendant, and it was owned by my favorite star.

Dammit, rip it off.

I reach up, then undo the clasp. I hold the pendant as the chain falls from my neck. Then I turn, intending to put the necklace into the small jewelry case I travel with.

But I don't. Instead, I drop it into the cup that serves as a holder for my toothbrush.

I stare at the cup—that's no place for such a lovely piece of jewelry. But I don't retrieve it. Instead, I strip off my clothes, leaving them in a pile on the floor as I head into the bedroom, trying not to think about how strange I feel.

No. Not strange.

Wrong.

I shiver, then close my eyes, trying to shake off this rawness. I rummage through the dresser into which I'd tossed the contents of my suitcase, then tug on my favorite leggings. I'm in the process of putting on the ratty concert tee I always travel with for lounging when I hear it—a soft, rhythmic thumping that seems to be coming from all around me.

The tee is covering my face, and I yank it down, then

stand, turning in a circle as I try to find the source of the sound. I tell myself it's Damien. He's decided to chop up an apple, or he went outside to deal with some pipe or something that needs to be banged back into place.

But that's just me making up stories.

I know where the sound is coming from. *I know everything about this house. Which means I also know that there's no place to hide. No place at all.*

A cold shiver races through me, and I blink, trying to recall my last thought. Something about the house. But the thought is gone. Out of reach, like the string of a helium balloon drifting higher and higher, just beyond my grasp.

That doesn't matter, though. Whatever the thought, I still know where it was leading —*the attic.*

I look up, and I know I'm right. Whatever that thumping is, it's coming from above me.

I hurry out of the bedroom to the small hallway with the large storage closet. I yank the door open, then sigh with relief when I look up and see the string hanging down. The strange thumping has stopped, but that doesn't matter. I want to know what—or who—is up there.

I tug on the string, then cough as a cloud of dust descends on me. I brush it off, unfold the stairs, and eagerly make the climb.

The attic is large, and the scent of age and decay fills the air. I pause at the top of the ladder, my head and shoulders in the space while the rest of my body waits below the attic floor.

"Hello?" Immediately, I feel foolish. Of course, no one is here. It's just old house noises.

And yet, I can't shake the feeling that someone—or something—is watching.

Get a grip!

With that quick and dirty pep talk, I climb the rest of the way into the dark space, then straighten when I realize I can stand without bumping my head. The room is dim, but a few shafts of light stream in through two small, dusty windows. My eyes adjust, and I see the single light bulb suspended from the ceiling. I reach up to pull the cord, surprised to find that the bulb still works, and it casts the room in a dim, yellow light, illuminating the dancing dust motes.

Discarded furniture hides beneath dusty sheets, and boxes are stacked precariously against the walls. One dusty trunk stands out by virtue of not being covered. I move carefully to it, fearful of rotting boards. The attic feels heavy with secrets. As if it's been waiting for someone—*for me*—to uncover them.

I shiver, then order myself to get a grip.

The trunk is brown, its leather straps cracked and worn. I see a lock and silently curse, only to realize that the padlock is hanging open. I take it off, then draw a deep breath, this moment feeling somehow solemn. Then I open the latches and lift the lid.

Inside, carefully folded and surprisingly well-preserved, is a collection of clothing. Evening gowns, silk gloves, delicate scarves. My breath catches. These aren't just any clothes. These belonged to Vivien Lorainne.

I reach in, gently pulling out a rose-gold gown that I remember from *Starlight Serenade.* My breath catches as I recall the scene in the grand ballroom with Vivien standing tall in that dress. Elegant. Timeless. Alive.

The unease I'd felt earlier is back, sharper now, like the point of a knife pressing against my skin. I lift a gown from the trunk, its cream-colored fabric shimmering faintly in the dim light. As I hold it up, a sudden chill races down my spine, and I spin around in time to see a drape flutter to the floor, revealing a dresser with an attached mirror.

She's there.

Vivien.

She's looking straight at me. And all around, I hear overlapping whispers of her voice. And then, cutting through the chaos, one phrase rises clear and sharp, cutting through me like ice:

"You shouldn't have come."

10

———

Damien paced in front of the living room fireplace, the crackling fire providing the only illumination. The scent of burning cedar filled the space. A scent he usually relished, but which tonight felt heavy. Cloying.

He'd hoped to spend the rest of the day after brunch with Nikki, enjoying a walk on the island or just lazing in the cottage's backyard, soaking up the sun, reading, talking. And, hopefully, shaking off this strange sense of discontent that had gotten its claws in him.

Instead, he'd spent the day alone while Nikki poked through boxes of Vivien Lorainne's dusty wardrobe. He didn't begrudge her the excitement of finding such a treasure, but dammit, he'd wanted to spend time with his wife. Now it was well after dark, and he'd barely seen her.

He ran his fingers through his hair, frustrated with both her and himself. She was excited by her find, and he was acting like a teenage boy whose feelings got hurt when his girlfriend decided to go shopping with friends instead of spending the day with him.

He stopped in front of the fireplace, then leaned forward, his hands on the mantle. It was dotted with framed photographs, and he picked one up—a sepia photo of Vivien Lorainne standing on a movie set, resplendent in a slinky gown that clung to every curve. Her luminous smile hinted at secrets, her gaze sultry and knowing.

He held the frame with one hand, the fingertip of his other tracing over her face. She was so beautiful. So like Nikki.

He felt a pressure in his chest. The kind of physical sensation he still felt when his wife walked into a room. When she smiled at him. When she looked at him with those beautiful eyes, unzipped her dress, and let it fall to the floor.

Nikki.

Vivien.

He pushed down a wave of unease. The house seemed unnervingly quiet, and the air felt heavy, pressing down like a weight on his chest.

With a small shiver, he looked down at the photo again, noticing the way she seemed to be looking right at him from the corner of her eye. He blinked, then looked again, something gnawing at him that he couldn't quite name.

The faint creak of a floorboard broke his thoughts, and he looked up to see Nikki standing in the doorway. His breath caught, and for a moment, it was as if the photograph had come to life. She was wearing the dress—the very same dress Vivien wore in the photo. And with her hair styled in soft waves, the resemblance was striking.

Her mouth curved into the kind of smile that promised all sorts of naughty things, and he felt himself go hard as she moved toward him, the satiny rose-gold fabric clinging to her curves.

She was stunning. Sensual. Sexual. Magnetic. *And not entirely herself.*

The thought came unbidden, and he tried to push it away as she stopped in front of him, her teasing smile drawing him closer.

"What do you think?" Her voice was low and breathy. She did a slow turn for him, then cast him a coy glance as her fingers stroked the snake bracelet, its emerald eyes winking hypnotically in the firelight.

Damien swallowed hard. "That gown was in the attic?"

She nodded, her fingertips lightly brushing her own skin as she traced the low-cut bodice. "It was like it was waiting for me." Her teeth grazed her lower lip, her eyes hot on his. "You like it?"

He broke eye contact to let his gaze rake over her, relishing the familiar heat that flared inside him. There'd never been a moment when he didn't want her. When she didn't make him burn. His skin. His blood. His soul.

And there'd never been a moment when he hadn't been willing to go into that flame with her.

But now…

Right then he feared that if he touched her they would both get scalded. But damned if he could help himself.

Almost as if he was watching himself in a dream, he moved closer, stopping only when he was right in front of her, so close he could feel the need radiating off her. So close that they were breathing the same air.

"Damien," she whispered, then tugged something from his hand. *The photo.* He'd forgotten that he'd been holding it, and the look on Nikki's face as she studied the picture unnerved him. Because she didn't look at all unsettled by the fact that she was wearing the dress pictured in the photo. On the contrary, the smile on her face was the kind that came at the conclusion of a long journey—when you're so close you can see the end.

But what the hell did that mean?

He shook his head, hating that he didn't understand. That he wasn't in control. Hating that it wasn't him she wanted but the damn dress and a life that didn't even exist anymore.

Someone else's life.

"What the fuck, Nikki?" The words snapped out, surprising him. *What the hell was happening?*

But the question was only inside him. Buried deep. And Damien had spent his entire life keeping parts of himself hidden. He could keep that questioning part locked up, too. Hell, yes, he could...

"Sweetheart, what's wrong?"

She met his eyes, her forehead furrowed with confusion. Slowly, she traced the edge of the frame with her fingertip. "She looks so glamorous," she said, her eyes dipping to the photo, then back up at him, her mouth curved into a frown. "Do I look glamorous?"

"You know you do."

"Sexy?" She took a step closer.

"Hell, yes."

She rose up on her tiptoes, then whispered in his ear. "That's what you want, isn't it? Sex? Heat?" Her lips brushed his ear. "Someone who can get you off? Someone who can make you forget?"

His spine and his cock went rigid at her words. *Desire,* he thought. *And danger.*

"Nikki—"

"It's okay." Her teeth grazed her lower lip before she offered him a seductive smile. "I know you're only using me. You've only ever used me."

She pushed the photo back into his hand, then traced her fingers over his shoulders and down his arms. "I'm only using you, too. You know that, Damien," she whispered as she slid one hand down to cup his cock. "You've always known that."

"Nikki." He could barely get her name out. His breath had gone ragged. His skin hot with need, his cock hard. He wanted to take her, to fuck her, to punish the bit—

No.

The word cut through his thoughts, and for a moment he felt in control of himself again. He'd never once used that word to her. This wasn't him. *This wasn't him.*

But the thought vanished almost as quickly as it had come, replaced by the truth of her words. They did use each other. They always had. Because that's what they were. That's *who* they were. That's how they'd saved each other. That was the deep, bright kernel of their love. The source that fed the intensity of their passion.

And now the little bitch was making a mockery of it. Who the hell did she think she was—

No. No, dammit, no!

Cold horror ran through his veins, and as he lurched backward the realization flashed inside him like a beacon.

Something was in him.

He dropped the photo, the sharp crash of shattering glass burying the thought. He bent to pick up the broken frame, then cursed as he sliced his thumb on a shard.

"Hush," she said, sidling up to him as he stood. He started to turn away, intending to search out a bandage, but she caught his arm, holding him in place. He froze, watching as she bent down, then picked up another shard.

She studied it, her head tilting as she considered it.

"No," he whispered as she put the edge of the glass

against the heel of her hand. He thought of the scars on her legs. Of the need she'd spent most of her life battling. "No," he whispered. "Nikki, no."

She lifted her head and met his eyes. Then she dropped the shard, and for a moment he thought he saw both clarity and fear reflected on her face. Then it vanished, and she was someone else again. Vivien, Nikki, he didn't know. All he knew was that she was close enough that he felt her heat. Close enough to lift his thumb to her lips. And then, with a soft moan, to lick the blood off.

He ought to be disgusted or afraid.

He wasn't. He felt hot. Wild. *Aroused.*

"Nikki," he whispered, as wildfire seemed to fill him. "What are you—" But he didn't finish the question. How could he when he was too mesmerized by this woman who now took his thumb and painted her lips with his blood?

This woman who leaned in and kissed him so that he tasted the salty sweetness. So that he felt the surge of an unfamiliar, dangerous passion.

This woman who wasn't his wife, because he was no longer Damien. He was need and longing.

Most of all, he was a desire so potent it could only be quenched with blood.

11

Nikki's lips crashed against his in a kiss that was fierce, predatory, and tinged with the metallic taste of blood. A blood that seemed to cut through him like fire, making his head swim and his cock strain against his jeans. He felt wild. Lost. And as their tongues warred—wild and desperate—her fingers tangled in his hair, pulling him closer as if through the force of sheer will she could make their bodies one.

Nikki.

The taste of her. The heat of her. He couldn't remember ever wanting her more, and yet a voice in the back of his head cried out that this was wrong. Off.

Dangerous.

He didn't care.

This wasn't Nikki—somehow he knew that. The woman who burned so hot against him wasn't his wife. She wasn't the woman who knew him, loved him, matched him in every way.

And yet she was...

And oh, god, how he craved her. Burned for her.

He tried to fight the urge. Tried to tell himself something was wrong. Terribly, horribly wrong. But that thought was only in his head. The rest of him—body, soul—craved her. Wanted her. Needed her.

The rest of him felt power and lust and longing surging through his veins.

The rest of him would beat the doubts down.

And, yes, he would have her.

"Damien."

His name was like a switch, shutting off the irritating thoughts, leaving him free to crave, to touch, to need.

And, yes, to succumb.

With a low groan, he pulled her to him again, his mouth capturing hers as her hands roamed his body, her touch frantic and desperate. Her nails scraped his scalp, sending sparks down his spine as her tongue invaded his mouth, coaxing and demanding all at once. She pressed against him, their bodies aligning perfectly, and he could feel the heat of her through the thin fabric of her dress.

A stab of resistance rose inside him, desperate for an explanation. Fighting the manic energy that was coursing through both of them.

But he shoved it back down. He didn't want answers—*he did! He did!*—all he wanted was her. Her body and that primal need that was impossible to ignore.

Her scent filled his senses—a mix of her familiar perfume and something darker, muskier. Something that clouded his judgment like a drug.

No.

Roughly, he pushed away, then drew in a breath as a moment of clarity surged through him. *This*, he thought. *Hang on to this.*

But then her lips found his, and his determination shattered as she kissed him harder. Deeper. Hungrier.

He reached behind her, finding the zipper, tugging the dress down, leaving the vintage garment discarded on the floor and kicking it aside so that he could throw her naked onto the couch, lost in her laughter. A raw sound, like a woman who'd just won a battle.

Well, maybe she had.

Then she reached up and grabbed at his shirt, ripping it open, popping buttons with an urgency that bordered on violence. Her lips left his, trailing along his jaw to his neck, her teeth grazing his skin and sending jolts of pleasure and pain through him.

He drew back, then stood, wanting to see her there, laid out on the couch, naked and ready for him, her lips darkened with blood, smears staining her skin as she touched herself. As she spread her legs, revealing the scars on her inner thighs.

"Please," she whispered, and he came to her, leaning over to kiss her, but she caught his hand, then drew his thumb over those scars before locking her eyes on his.

"Nikki—" His voice broke, low and raw.

But she only smiled, then drew her fingers over the scars. Over the blood, but whether she was trying to draw it in or erase it, he didn't know. All he knew was the heady scent—metallic and sharp and electric.

All he knew was the way the air crackled between them, charged with something wild and hot. Something he couldn't name but desperately wanted. Something he knew he should run from, but he couldn't. He could only move forward, drawn as if by a magnet.

There's iron in blood.

She reached out her hand, then drew him to her,

spreading her legs. "Please," she whispered, her voice thick with something primal. "I need you. It's been too long. Far, far too long."

A voice inside screamed that he needed to run. Needed to find answers.

Needed to find his wife.

But then she opened her eyes, and all he saw was Nikki. She reached for his hand, then stood up, pulling him toward her as she looked at him with hunger-filled eyes. "Fuck me," she whispered, her fingers tugging at the button of his jeans.

Firelight danced across her face, highlighting the wildness in her expression, making him wild, too. Her lips found his neck, her teeth grazing and biting as her hands worked frantically to shove the jeans down over his hips.

Yes. Oh, god, yes.

He wanted her. Craved her.

Not like this. This wasn't right.

But it felt right. So damn right. His wife. His woman.

His Vivien.

No.

He jerked back, his body desperate for release, his mind spinning.

She was Nikki.

She was his wife.

Then take her. Prove it. Claim her. Make her yours.

Yes. Dammit, yes.

With two fluid movements, he kicked his jeans the rest of the way off, then pulled them both down to the couch. She straddled him, her smile one of pure victory. He didn't care. He no longer knew if this was right or wrong. He didn't even know who he was. Who she was.

All he knew was *her.*

That she was his, and he had to have her. Had to take

her if he was ever going to find his sanity again, because the feel of her—the heat, the pressure, the desperation—was undoing him.

"Yes," she said, her hands pinned on his shoulders. She offered him a smile of victory before her lips descended on his, fierce and demanding. He gripped her hips, his fingers digging into her flesh as she moved against him, their bodies colliding with a force that was both passionate and brutal.

"You're mine," she whispered, her voice a rasp. Her nails raked down his chest, leaving faint red trails in their wake. "Say it. Say you're mine."

"I—" His words dissolved into a groan as she ground herself against him.

Her hands cupped his face. "Say it."

"Yours." The word tumbled from his lips. "Goddammit, you know I'm yours."

A smile curled her lips, but it was wrong. *It wasn't Nikki.* And that realization clawed at the edges of his mind even as his body betrayed him, responding to her with a ferocity he couldn't control.

Nikki, Vivien, Carlton, Damien.

He didn't know any of them. Right then, he didn't care.

They moved together, their rhythm wild and frantic. Her nails dug into his back, her teeth grazing his shoulder, her breath hot against his ear. He wanted her. Needed her. And he hated himself for it. Because, dammit, the woman he was fucking wasn't Nikki. Not really.

And what the hell did that say about him?

12

———

Damien stood outside the Pavilion Hotel, the night wrapping around him like a too-tight jacket. The rhythmic thrum of the nearby surf blended with the melodic tangle of voices drifting from the bar. Normal sounds—ordinary, even. And he wondered how the world around him could go on as usual when his own world was spiraling into danger and mystery.

He drew a breath, part of him wanting to turn away. To forget about this appointment. To ignore the answers he so desperately needed.

To go back to Nikki.

Is she Nikki? Is she even still your wife?

For three days now, he'd been asking himself that horrible question. Ever since the night with the dress. With the blood.

Nothing felt real. Three children. Years together.

And a primal connection that he'd never felt with anyone other than Nikki.

She was his, dammit. *His.*

But right then, he was terrified that she wasn't. Not anymore.

He felt his hands tighten into fists as his body tensed. But who was he supposed to fight? Nikki? The house? The memory of Vivian Lorainne?

And where the hell could he go—where could he take her? They couldn't outrun this nightmare. No matter how much he might want to, somehow, he knew that he had to stay.

Had to fight. Not his wife, but the ... *thing* ... that had seduced her.

He shivered, fear as cold as ice trailing down his spine. *He couldn't lose her. He couldn't.*

And yet, dammit, he was terrified that he already had.

The thought sent a fresh wave of tension through him. He was a man who prided himself on control. Keeping it. Enforcing it. He was Damien Fucking Stark, but for the last three days, he sure as hell hadn't felt like it.

Not with his wife turning into another person. Wearing only Vivien Lorainne's clothes. Styling her hair as the star had done. Even mimicking Vivien's makeup.

And, yes, maybe he could have handled that—convinced himself it was only a way for Nikki to amuse herself, or chalked it up to boredom on the island and taken her home—*if* that had been the only thing going on.

But it wasn't. She'd grown distant. Cold.

Different.

In the space of three days, she'd become a woman he didn't know. A terrifying thought because he knew Nikki as well as he knew himself. Or, at least, he thought he did.

Was he even himself anymore? He wasn't sure. But he knew one thing for certain—the woman in his bed wasn't Nikki anymore.

Yes, she still came to him. Yes, she still touched him. Stroked him. Whispered that she wanted him. And, damn him, he responded, pushed by a need so powerful it felt like it was coming from outside him. Taking her hard. Taking her fast. Begging her with every touch and every kiss and every thrust deep inside her to tell him what was wrong. Why she'd withdrawn.

Why she was losing herself to a murdered movie star?

She never gave him a clue.

She gave him sex. And she gave him silence.

She gave him Vivien Lorainne.

But when she looked at him, he saw something beneath that facade. Something cold and calculating.

Something that scared the hell out of him.

"*Dammit.*" The word came out hard, lingering in air that seemed to carry a strange tension. He drew in a breath to calm the storm building inside him, then let it out slowly. He wanted his wife back. And for that, he needed answers. So he'd come here to talk to the only person he knew who might be able to help.

Determined, he squared his shoulders, then took a step forward. Then another, and another after that, until he was inside the hotel and saw Franklin Hart sitting at one of the tables in the lobby bar.

"Dr. Hart. Thank you for meeting me," Damien said after he'd shook hands with the man. He settled into his own seat as a waiter hurried over with a Scotch.

"Please. Call me Franklin. And you'll allow me to call you Damien?"

"Of course," Damien said. He hadn't noticed it after the auction, but there was something about the man he didn't care for. Something about the way he held himself. The way he looked at Damien but didn't quite meet his eyes. But that didn't matter now. Franklin was his only resource, and Damien was enough of a negotiator to know when he did—and, more importantly, when he didn't—hold the upper hand.

Franklin leaned back in his chair, and Damien felt the man's eyes on him. Studying him. "You said you needed my professional opinion," he finally said, "but beyond that, I'm at a loss. Are we talking matters of the psyche or the occult?"

Damien took a sip of the Scotch, letting it sit on his tongue, relishing the burn, and giving himself a few precious seconds before he had to speak his fears aloud. And, in so doing, move them from imagination to reality.

"Both," he finally said. "Though, to be honest, I hope this falls within the purview of psychology. If I can walk away from this table knowing that my fears are all in my head, you'll have made me a very happy man."

"I see," Franklin said, though of course he didn't. Not yet. "Then let us keep an open mind as we chat. Tell me why you called me. Leave nothing out, even if you believe it was only in your mind."

It was harder to start talking than he'd anticipated. After all, he'd spent his life building walls, locking his vulnerabilities away where no one could see them. But now, with Nikki slipping through his fingers and that damn house breathing down his neck, he needed to show his cards. Because Nikki's sanity—hell, maybe her life—depended on it.

And so he began. He told Franklin everything. From the original impulse to buy the house to the strange connection Nikki seemed to have with the place. He told Franklin about the violent—even bloody—sex. About the way the house seemed to whisper.

He couldn't explain it, but something about the place felt off. Wrong in a way that defied logic or reason. He wasn't a man who believed in ghosts or curses. But if the house wasn't haunted, it was doing a damn good impression of it.

Franklin's expression barely changed as Damien laid it all out, but Damien caught the slight tilt of his head, the way his eyes narrowed just a fraction. Observing. Analyzing. The look of a man who could see straight through bullshit.

Damien kept going, telling Franklin about the changes to his wife. The strange obsession with Vivien Lorainne. The distance. "She goes out without telling me where she's going. Comes back with nothing but nonsense."

"Nonsense?"

"Trinkets. Little things. Nothing that matters."

Franklin hummed thoughtfully. "And what do you think it means?"

An impotent rage rose inside him. "I haven't got a fucking clue. All I know is that she's not Nikki anymore." He closed his eyes. Tried to tamp down the fury ... and the fear. "I need you, sir. I need you to tell me how to bring her back." He shook his head, then sighed. "I sound insane."

"You don't," Franklin said smoothly. "But you do sound like a man who's troubled. And I certainly see why."

Damien closed his eyes, then drew a breath. "It's the house, isn't it? It feels ... wrong. Like it's alive. Like it's seeping into her, changing her." He let out a sharp breath. "I know how ridiculous that sounds, but I can't shake it."

God, he sounded unhinged.

Franklin nodded slowly, his expression unreadable. "You're worried, of course. And it's true—houses can carry energy. Memories. It's not unheard of."

"So you're saying—"

"*No*," Franklin said firmly. He sat back. "Your house isn't haunted, Damien. Of that, I'm certain. What I'm saying is that when you hear hoof beats, think horses, not zebras."

"What do you mean?"

Franklin steepled his fingers. "You know I'm interested in the occult, so a haunted house is not something that I would dismiss without certainty. But despite the stories over the years, there hasn't been any credible indication of a haunting at your cottage."

Damien thought of the strange noises. Nikki's behavior. The stories that Franklin was so easily dismissing.

Franklin laughed. "You're thinking too loud, my friend. Come on, if the house were truly haunted, don't you think someone in my position would know it?"

Damien dragged his fingers through his hair. "Fine. But what's your point?"

"I'm saying that when someone feels trapped, they often act out. So you tell me. Which is more likely— that Nikki is working through some sort of frustration or that some dark presence in your house is manipulating her?"

"You think Nikki feels trapped?" Damien shook his head. "No. I'm sorry, but you're wrong. You don't know my wife. You don't know *us.*"

"Perhaps not," Franklin said. "But I know how stress can impact a person. How changes in environment can be a trigger. And I also know a bit about your wife's history. She was very brave to talk publicly about her history with cutting, but it *is* her history."

Damien tightened his hand around his Scotch, not sure if that was to center himself or to have it at the ready in case he decided to throw it. He kept his voice steady as he said, very slowly and very clearly, "What exactly are you saying?"

"I think it's very likely that Nikki is having an affair."

Damien went completely still. "No." The word was immediate. Firm.

And yet...

"No," he repeated.

Franklin tilted his head. "You sound certain."

"Of course I'm certain," Damien snapped.

"It's just that—" Franklin shook his head. "Never mind."

Something cold and dangerous seemed to writhe in Damien's gut. "Tell me."

Silence lingered.

"*Goddammit.* Tell me."

Franklin lifted his hands as if in surrender. "It's just that at the gala, I saw her talking to a man. I spoke to him later. Greg was his name. But I know people, Damien. I'm trained to look at people and to truly see them. And Greg wasn't there for the gala. He was there for her."

Damien stared at him, the knot in his chest tightening. "What the hell am I supposed to do with that?"

"You need to talk to her. Bring this out into the open. Let her know you see the changes. That you're aware. If it's an affair, confronting her will force her to face it. If it's something else, it might be enough to snap her out of it. But you can't keep ignoring it."

Damien's stomach twisted. "And if you're wrong?"

"Then you have ruled out one cause for this new distance between you. You talk, and you rebuild."

Rebuild.

How was that word even in his vocabulary where Nikki was concerned?

Dammit, he wasn't going to lose her. Not to a house, not to some asshole named Greg. Not to anything.

But as he walked back to the cottage an hour later, a whisper of doubt coiled through him, dark and insidious.

Was she even still his to bring back?

It's late. The house is silent, except for the faint creaks of wood expanding and settling, as if the house itself is breathing. I sit curled up in the armchair near the window, the dim light of a single lamp casting long shadows across the room.

I pull my legs up to my chest, resting my chin on my knees. *Craving. Needing.*

Blood.

I think about the blood. The way we'd been last night.

Not last night. Days ago.

Time … time isn't the same anymore.

I squeeze my eyes tight, forcing the thought away. All these strange thoughts in my head lately. I don't want the thoughts. I only want the memory of Damien. Of how it had felt. Raw and unrestrained, as if something primal had taken over both of us. Something wild and wonderful.

Something terrifying.

No. Not terrifying. Primal. Necessary.

I crave it even now. It should have left me sated, fulfilled. Instead, I feel … restless. Unsettled.

As if I'm not myself. As if my desire has a dangerous edge.

What is happening?

I close my eyes and breathe deeply, trying to calm the erratic thudding of my heart. But the calm doesn't come. Instead, I feel a strange sense of heaviness, like dark fingers pressing against my skin, holding me down. I want to get up. I want Damien.

I want to curl into his arms, to feel the safety and love that only he can provide.

He doesn't love you. He despises you. Despises what you've become.

No.

I scream the word, but there is no sound. I try to get out

of the chair, but I can't move. I'm frozen, pinned in place by an unseen force. I'm stroking the snake bracelet, the motion soothing, and when I'm calm enough, I look around. My eyes stop at the small table beside the chair, where the journal sits. Its cover is pristine now, unmarked. No ouroboros. No initials.

I reach for it, my fingers brushing over the smooth leather. A shiver runs down my spine as the memory of the shifting passages sends a chill through me. I want to throw it across the room. This horrible, wrong thing.

But instead, I flip open the cover and, again, begin to read.

The entries start out mundane. Notes about Vivien's day-to-day life. Tea with Carlton. A meeting with her agent. But as I turn the pages, the letters begin to blur, the ink shifting and swimming on the paper. I blink, my breath catching as the words reshape themselves into something darker:

Carlton swears Basil speaks to him in whispers. That he hears the voice even in his dreams. He insists Basil is more than flesh and blood. That he is strong. Inescapable. I'm scared. Scared of my own husband. And yet I don't understand why. I only know that he's changed.

I shudder, my grip on the journal tightening. My eyes dart to the next page, and I watch, mesmerized, as the ink ripples again before settling into stark, black words:

These pages are tainted—I am certain of it. I should stop writing in this journal, and yet I can't seem to do so. It's as if I'm compelled to record my thoughts. To spill out my soul. I only hope that by doing so I am not bleeding out.

My thoughts go again to Damien. To the blood. To the need. To the passion, raw and primal that played out between us.

Bleeding out...

Yes, that's what it feels like. Not blood, but my soul.

Damien!

The cry rips through my mind in one moment of pure, perfect terror. I love him. I need him.

I need him to save me.

But Damien isn't here.

Basil is, though. Basil is everywhere.

And Basil loves me.

13

———

Damien walked back to the cottage, the light of the full moon casting long, sharp shadows that seemed to follow him, flickering and stretching as if alive. He moved slowly, replaying the conversation with Franklin over and over, as if on an infinite loop.

An affair.

Cheating.

Betrayal.

He didn't want to believe it. Hell, he couldn't believe it. Not Nikki. It wasn't possible. He knew her as well as he knew himself. Trusted her more than he'd ever trusted anyone.

It wasn't possible.

It wasn't.

And yet with each block he walked—with each inch closer to the cottage—a tiny tendril of doubt expanded, growing into a wide, curling ribbon, as dark and insidious as a coiled basilisk just waiting to strike.

You've been betrayed before.

True, though not by her. The thought twisted through him, raw and grating—*Not that he knew of, anyway.*

But he knew the feel of betrayal. The bitter taste of it.

He shuddered as the sharp screech of a bird echoed through the darkness, underscoring the thought.

She's changed. Admit it, Damien. Your wife has changed.

His skin seemed to prickle in the wake of that horrible truth. She *was* changing. Becoming withdrawn. Sliding into her strange fascination with Vivien Lorainne. Leaving the cottage alone for her excursions into town, only to return with silly, foolish purchases.

An alibi. The voice in his mind was harsh. Firm. *The silly little purchases were nothing more than cover for her visits to him. The little bitch. The cunning whore.*

Bile rose in his throat as he shuddered at the words, his hands clenching into tight fists as some buried part of himself tried to will the dark thoughts away. Thoughts that weren't his. Could never be his.

And yet there they were. In his head, feeling real and right and raw.

Logical.

Aligning perfectly with the evidence.

And so desperately, horribly wrong. The little bitch thought she could get away with it? That she could—

No.

Focus. Dammit, focus!

He stopped dead on the sidewalk, his hands clenched into fists at his sides. He had to think. Had to make his thoughts move.

His thoughts.

Because something was wrong. Terribly wrong. And it wasn't Nikki having an affair, because she wasn't. She wouldn't. He knew that. He *knew* it.

But something *was* wrong. And not just in his head. She'd pulled away—cloaked herself in Vivien Lorainne's shadow. And he had no idea how to bring her back.

But it was him, too. He felt raw. Exposed. As if a part of him had been peeled away, leaving him open to every doubt, every whisper of inadequacy. Every flicker of rage.

She'd done this to him. He loved her too much, too hard.

She'd made him weak. Foolish.

Yeah, well fuck that. Fuck doubt. Fuck weakness.

Fuck her.

But even as that thought ricocheted through his head, another softer voice seemed to speak in the darkness of his soul. *Hold on. Hold tight. It isn't real. This isn't right.*

He cringed, trying to block the rhythmic, almost singsong words. Instead, he focused on the cottage just half a block away. The sight of it—quaint and charming beneath the moonlight—only stoked his anger. He'd bought it for her. For Nikki. He'd thought it would be a gift, a retreat. Instead, it had become a prison. For both of them.

By the time he reached the gate, his blood was boiling. He couldn't articulate the source of his wrath, but it didn't matter. He knew—somehow, he just *knew*—that he was right about her. About her deceit. Her betrayals.

Every kiss had been a slap. Every fuck a joke.

But why, why, why?

The question seemed to pound at his skull with ineffectual baby fists. No power. Only incomprehensible mews that quickly died in his mind to lay buried beneath the bitter red of betrayal and heartache.

Who the hell did she think she was, cheating on him? On him!

She'd made a mockery of him, dammit. And he wasn't a man who would stand for that.

By the time he crossed the short distance from the gate to the door, he could feel the blood pounding in his veins, so intense he could imagine its sweet, coppery taste. Something cold and slippery coiled in his gut, craving the blood, urging him forward.

Despite hands shaking with fury, he finally managed to slide the key into the lock and then open the door. The air inside seemed heavy. Oppressive. As if dark things were hiding in shadowy corners. As if the weight of everything in the cottage was bearing down on him.

He moved further inside, his steps slow. Almost silent. Had to catch her in the act. Had to show the bitch who was boss.

The living area was dark, as was the kitchen. But he saw a faint glow in the hallway that led to the bedroom, and he moved in that direction, stalking his prey.

His skin tingled, his body on fire. A dark power raged through him, black as night, breathing fire into him. Strengthening him. Readying him for what was to come.

No. Not strength. Something else.

Something else was twisting inside him.

He fought to grab hold of his thoughts, but they seemed to scurry away, almost as if in terror.

Terror. Oh, yes. The time for terror had come, slithering closer with every breath. And soon she would know the extent of his wrath—and the pain that accompanies a punishment rendered without the weakness of mercy and—

No!

"Nikki!"

It took more effort than anything he'd ever had to do to force the word to burst out of him, and yet he heard no sound. He was silenced. Trapped.

He? The voice slithered through his mind. *The "he" you*

used to be doesn't even exist anymore. It is only I. The dark. The serpent.

The Basilisk.

Somewhere in a deep, dark hole, the soul that had once been Damien railed against the bars of an invisible prison, trying to escape. Trying to understand.

Then he saw her.

She stood in the middle of the room, looking at him with terror in her eyes, and he felt himself go hard when she parted her lips and whispered his name. *"Damien."*

"Nikki."

It was more of a growl than a word, and though he felt the coarseness of it in his throat, he knew he hadn't spoken. More, he knew he wasn't the only creature looking through his eyes at the woman standing before him. A stunning woman whose hair fell in waves to her shoulders. Whose body was clad in what must have been a scandalous evening gown decades ago, the thin material hugging her body in a way that made his chest tighten— with lust, with fear, and with something else he couldn't name.

Desire. Greed. Need. And more. So much more.

It's fury, too, and it's beating down on you. Can't you taste it, Damien? She's cheating. The little bitch is cheating on you. You!

She thinks she can cheat on the likes of Damien Stark and get away with it. Tell her. Show her. Prove to her she can't get away with it.

Ice water flooded his veins, the strength of it pushing him forward even as she ran toward him, her mascara running in dark streaks over her cheeks. "It's Basil. Damien, please. The journal. It's Basil. It's Basil, and I—"

She lurched back as if something invisible had grabbed her from behind. He watched, feeling a cold nothingness mixed with glee as he saw her stumble—as he realized that she was going to fall. *Served the cheating little whore right.*

Then she was on the floor, the hem of her gown ripped from where she had caught it on the heel of her shoe, her temple bleeding from where she'd slammed it against the edge of the dresser.

He caught the smell of blood, threw his head back, and roared, the sound raw and primal. *And not his. This wasn't him. Dear god, this wasn't him.*

Oh, but it is. You are we and we are I. And she will get what she deserves. And the little adulterer deserves pain. And she sure as hell doesn't deserve us.

He kept his eyes on Nikki, his heart pounding in his chest as he willed himself to run to her. To touch her. To make sure she was alright.

But he couldn't move. Something held him back. Invisible arms seemed to tighten around his chest, holding him still as he struggled to breathe.

"Nikki!" The scream ripped out of him—or tried to. In truth, it was barely a whisper.

She has to die for us. The little bitch cheated, remember? She has to die. And her death will bring us more power. You will be more than a king. We will be more than a god. Ambition, Damien. We will burn across the world and feed your ambition. You have always sought power—and the little bitch has been keeping you down. Making you soft. Making you weak.

The words twisted in his head. In his gut. "No." Somehow, he managed to rip the word out, but the rest was trapped in his head. Trapped with the basilisk. With the demon.

Fool. You say she is your everything. That she is your ambition. That without her you are nothing? You are weak. But once she is dead, you will learn. You will learn the meaning of power.

Terror, cold and vile, ricocheted through him.

Fight. Need to fight. Need to *do*.

But do what? Fight how?

There's a clue. Something he was missing. Find the clue. Think, dammit. Somewhere, there has to be a clue.

Has to die, has to die, the pretty, pretty girl has to die.

For us.

For us.

For us.

His body lurched, and something cold and dark seemed to fill him, a strange calmness settling over him. He shifted, his focus on the woman who called herself wife. The woman he'd fucked so many times. The woman who was cheating on him.

Greg, the voice said. *You know she is cheating with a little prick named Greg.*

"Bitch." The word was only a whisper, but he saw the impact on her. Saw the terror fill her eyes ... and he felt the stronger seeing it. He fed on it. Needed it. Craved it.

"Damien, please." Her voice was soft, laced with that erotic tinge of fear. He could see her looking around the room, trying to find a way to escape. But there was no way out. No way past him. No possibility that she could get by without him catching her. Hurting her.

Without him savoring the pain and glorying in the blood.

She was right to be afraid. Death was scary for those to whom it meant something. But her sacrifice would not be forgotten. He had to do it. Had to kill her. If he was going to become, he had to kill her.

We have to kill her.

It will be the final act in becoming. Her death will

destroy his soul. Without his soul, he will follow us anywhere.

Us.

We.

One.

A soft ripple—almost too gentle to be noticed—moved through him. *Think. Learn.*

But there was nothing left to learn. Nothing left to do. *He was the demon, and the demon was him. And that was the way it should be. The way it had always been. With Carlton and with those before him. Now, with Damien and those who would come after.*

No. No. There was a way. He just had to figure it out. Because, dammit, there was a way. He was still himself. He could still hear his thoughts. He could still—

NO!

He felt something like fear skitter through him as understanding ripped through his mind. He was the demon, and the demon was him. And that was the key.

Relief swelled inside him, diluting the fear. *You want to merge with me, you son-of-a-bitch? Too bad you can't hide your secrets if you become me.*

He had a plan now. So long as he could stay strong, so long as he could fight the evil that had hijacked him, he could get them through this.

But that was the trick—staying strong. Staying alive.

He could. *He would.* Because he had to. For Nikki, he had to.

14

____

amien! Damien, please!

I try to cry out, but the voice is only in my head. He's walking toward me, this man who looks like Damien. Who *is* Damien.

And yet he isn't.

Basil.

The air presses against my skin, heavy and damp, as if it's trying to hold me in place. Damien moves toward me, his steps deliberate, his face twisted in a way I don't recognize, as if he's fighting something horrible.

As if he's fighting himself.

Another step. Then another. And still not a word. Nothing to let me know if he's still my husband. If he's Basil. Or if he's someone else.

Or something worse.

"Damien," I whisper, my voice trembling. My body feels frozen, locked between fear and disbelief. "Please, it's me."

But is it?

Fight, a voice in my head whispers. *Fight like I never did.*

I glance down at the bodice of the dress I'm wearing. I

reach up to touch the carefully styled waves that frame my face. I trace my finger over my lips, then look at my fingertip, now smeared with blood-red lipstick.

I don't remember. I don't have any memory of dressing this way, and I shift to the side so that I can see myself in the full-length mirror. It's me. *Thank god, it's me.*

And yet there's something else there, too. A shimmer. *Vivien.*

Help him fight. The voice is only in my head, and I tremble from the desperation and terror. *He is fighting. Help him. Don't let Basil win. Don't meet my fate.*

I release a slow breath as a small respite of calm washes over me, only to be ripped away by a new voice, dark and slithering. *Don't trust her. Nothing is what it seems.*

I don't know what to do. I don't know what to trust. I don't even know if the voices are real or if I'm going crazy.

All I can do is look to Damien—my life. My love. The only person I have ever fully trusted, yet right now, I can see the battle raging inside him, and I know that he hears the voices, too. But he doesn't have Vivien. I don't know why, but I'm certain she's only with me, and that means he's fighting the oily darkness alone.

He takes an anguished step forward, his face a battle-field. I can see it—the man I love fighting against something dark and cruel. *Basil.*

Or maybe something worse.

His hands tremble at his sides, his jaw tight, his eyes flickering with rage and something else. Pain. Desperation.

And then he's himself.

For the briefest flash, his eyes soften, and I see the love that I know so well. "Take ... it ... off." The words seem forced out of him, as if he's fighting to speak, "Have to ... hurry... The sn—"

I scream, then scramble away as his body contorts even as he lunges for me. *No.* It isn't him who is after me, it's the creature inside him.

"*Go!*" The cry is ripped out of him, followed by a howl of pain that breaks my heart. But I go—I go like he said, racing to the bathroom, then slamming the door shut behind me as I try to figure out what I'm supposed to do.

Take it off.

Take what off?

Unsure, I strip off Vivien's gown and use the silky material to wipe off my make-up. Then I scrub my face until I can look in the mirror and see only me.

A hard knock sounds at the door, making the wood shake. "*Bitch!*"

It's Damien's voice, and yet it's not.

"Damien." I choke his name out past the tears, my voice trembling. "I don't know what to do. Please, please. I don't know what to do."

"*Nothing, you little bitch. I'm finally free of you.*" It's no longer his voice. It's cold and slithery, and I think I'm going to throw up because he's not Damien any longer and I don't know what to do. I don't know how to make it better. I don't know how to bring him back.

You can't. He's mine now. The voice is in my head. Not Vivien, but something vile and evil. *Soon, you will be, too.*

"No!" The scream bursts out of me even as I feel icy tendrils caressing my flesh, trying to squeeze inside me. To become me.

How? How do I make it stop? How do I wake up from this nightmare?

Take it off.

I remember Damien's words. He'd been fighting the demon to speak. To tell me something. *Take it off.*

But the only thing I'm wearing now is a bra. I'm not even wearing panties. Just my diamond earrings and the—

Yes!

The snake bracelet.

Even as the thought enters my mind, the door bursts open.

Damien.

It's him. The man who held me through my darkest moments. The man who loves me.

Then his face contorts and his fists clench, and I scurry back against the counter, terrified that this time the demon has won.

His hand tightens around the towel rack while the other clutches the door frame. "Hurry." His voice is rough. Guttural. "Get it off. Destroy it."

I look down at my wrist, where the snake bracelet gleams in the dim light. It feels hot, the metal burning into my skin as if it's trying to become a part of me. Panic rises in my chest as I claw at the clasp. "I can't," I say, my voice cracking. "Damien, I can't. It won't come off."

I meet his eyes—*Damien's eyes*. He's fighting, but I can see that he's losing. And somehow I know that if I can't get this bracelet off, then the demon will consume both of us. Worse, we'll be Vivien and Carlton all over again.

"I need your help," I whisper as I yank at the clasp. "I can't get it off." I hear the panic in my voice even as I try to uncoil the snake. As the bracelet begins to burn, growing hotter and hotter, until I can smell my own flesh searing.

"I don't know what to do," I say, my voice tight with pain. "I don't know—"

"*Now, dammit*" His voice is hard, filled with loss and regret. "I'm losing myself. It's consuming me. It's making me disappear."

My heart shatters. I want to run to him, to hold him, to kiss him until he's my Damien again. But this isn't a fairy tale. This is a nightmare. It's the freaking *Blair Witch Project* or *Saw* or—

Oh, god! It's *The Exorcist.*

I practically leap toward the counter. But he grabs the strap of my bra, yanking me back, my fingers only brushing the toothpaste cup on the counter.

But that's enough.

It topples, shattering on the tile floor and revealing the crucifix I'd dropped in there before.

I lunge for it, my hand closing around the cool metal as Damien's arm goes around my waist, pulling me toward him. Except he isn't Damien now. I know that.

More, I know that I have to bring him back. That I *can* bring him back.

With a cry, I bring the crucifix down on the bracelet. The clasp snaps, and the bracelet falls to the floor with a metallic clatter.

A deafening howl fills the room as a rush of icy wind swirls around us. I stagger back, watching in horror as the wind twists into a dark, writhing mass. It shoots out of the bathroom and into the bedroom. I hear glass shattering, then silence.

And then the sweetest sound I've ever heard—"Nikki?"

I whip around, tears streaming down my face. He's on his knees, his chest heaving. He rises up, his eyes meeting mine, clear and steady. And for the first time in days, I see him. Truly him.

And I know that I'm once again truly me.

I throw myself into his arms, and he wraps me in his embrace, holding me close, our hearts beating together, as one. As we should be.

15

———

"**N**ikki," he says when we finally pull out of our embrace, but not so much that we completely break contact. If I had my way, I'd never stop touching him again. "Oh, god, Nikki, I'm sorry. I'm so, so sorry."

"It's not your fault," I whisper. I'm kneeling on the bathroom floor, my palm stroking his cheek, my fingers tracing a pattern on his arm, as if any break in contact will start the nightmare all over again. "But I don't—I don't think I fully understand. Was it really Vivien? Was she inside me?"

"She was. Her essence, anyway." I see him shudder. "And Basil was, too. But only a tiny bit of him. She was protecting you. She saved you."

I shake my head. "*You* saved me. Or maybe you both did. But I saw you fighting. I could see that you were fighting the demon inside you."

I close my eyes, wishing I could block the memory. But at the same time I want to know. To understand. "Do you know what happened? How it happened? How we won?"

He lifts our joined hands and kisses my palm. "I know," he says. "I know, because it was still me. Somewhere inside, it was me." He cups my cheek, his face like a mask of pain. "I wanted to hurt you." His voice cracks, and I tighten my hands around his. "God, Nikki. Even as I tried to protect you, I wanted to hurt you."

The anguish in his voice squeezes my heart, and I brush a whisper-soft kiss over his lips. "No. Not you. The demon inside. And you fought it, Damien. You fought, and you won." I smile, just the tiniest tug at the corner of my mouth.

"I know," he says. "But if we hadn't won—baby, it would have been me who killed you."

Hot tears stream down my cheeks as I squeeze his hand. Hard. "No. Never. We both know you could never hurt me. And today you saved me."

He brushes a tear away with his fingertip, his touch so gentle I think I might start crying in earnest.

"We saved each other," he says. A hint of a smile touches his lips. "You had the strength to destroy the bracelet."

I glance at my now-bare wrist. "You understand all of it, don't you? About the bracelet. About Basil. You know because it was in you."

His throat moves as he swallows. "Yes." It's barely a whisper, yet the word is full of pain.

"Tell me."

It's clear he doesn't want to talk about it. But at the same time, I can see that he understands that I have to know. I watch as his shoulders sag, but he lifts his chin and meets my eyes, and I know he will tell me everything.

"The bracelet is ancient," he begins. "It was found centuries ago, and kept mostly in museums. The demon was already tied to it, and it manipulated those who came in contact with it, finally getting it in an auction and pushing Carlton to buy it for Vivien."

"Why her? Why them?"

"Carlton wanted power. Vivien had it—there's power that comes in being a star. But he was almost invisible next to her."

"He turned to the occult?"

Damien nods. "He brought forth the demon. Released it from the bracelet. He had no idea what kind of door he was opening. No idea that the demon would slide into the house as well. That it would manipulate him. Torment Vivien."

"A door to hell," I whisper, then shudder. "And Vivien's soul stayed on to fight it."

He nods as I blink back tears. "That's enough," I say. "I don't need to hear the rest. It's too sad, and I—"

"*Aaaaaeeeeeeeiiiiiiiii*"

I almost jump out of my skin at the loud, guttural cry. Damien leaps in front of me at the same time that Franklin fills the bathroom doorway, his arms out-stretched, palms on either side of the doorway. His clothes are covered with shards of glass, and I realize he must have been standing outside when the window blew out. His eyes burn blood-red, and his body is bloated like a caricature balloon filled to almost bursting.

His lip curls as his eyes meet Damien's. "You fool," he sneers in a low, grating voice that is barely recognizable as Franklin's. "You had the power inside you, and instead of embracing it, you fought it. Forced it out."

"Don't do this, Franklin," Damien says, his voice tight with control. "Fight it. We can help you."

"*Fool*. Don't you see that this was what I wanted all along?"

I grab Damien's hand and feel his grip tighten around mine.

"You weren't worthy to host the demon," Franklin continues, his grotesque form pulsating with the power of the evil inside him. "I am worthy."

"The hell you are," Damien says. "You're weak. You're a weak man looking for power, and you have no idea what that means."

"Oh, but I do. I planned for this. Manipulated it. And now I will become."

I watch, horrified, as he throws his head back, his body contorting as he cries out in a mix of pain and jubilation. Electricity—power—seems to skitter over his skin, leaving the scent of burning flesh as his clothes burn away. As his form contorts, stretching, growing, elongating.

I feel bile rise in my throat as I realize what's happening. "He's becoming the serpent." My words are barely a whisper, but from the way Damien squeezes my hand and shifts to put himself between me and the creature that was Franklin, I know he understands.

I also know that we're trapped. Franklin's growing, writhing form now fills the doorway, the acrid scent of burning flesh—of hell— fills the room. He snarls, showing fangs dripping with slime. "You will die slowly." The eyes, now slits, narrow even more as the body sways, the head turning to look at us in turn. "You will be the first meal in honor of my new life. My new power."

A forked tongue bursts from his mouth, darting across the small room to scrape my cheek. I scream and fall backward, only to slam the back of my head against the cabinetry.

"You're afraid. That's good. I feed on fear and blood."

He's fully Basil now, a basilisk. A demon. And when I look into his eyes, I see only death.

No. The word screams through my head. *No.* This can't be happening. We've been through so much. Survived so much. We expelled the demon from the house. From Damien. From the bracelet.

As if he's read my mind, Damien lurches across the small space, his hand closing over the dust that is the remnant of the bracelet. He snatches up the crucifix I'd dropped. And then, as the serpent slithers forward—as its jaw unhinges to reveal a dark, hellish maw—as I scream Damien's name, he thrusts his hand forward and shoves the crucifix down the beast's throat.

The serpent shrieks and the air fills with the stench of sulfur as the putrid flesh burns away to reveal Franklin's body, convulsing and screaming as he shivers and writhes as the demon fades. And then, with one final, piercing shriek, Franklin's body goes limp. His skin returns to a human color, and all that is left is the lifeless shell of a man who craved power, and lost himself to its dark, twisty depths.

"*Nikki.*"

In one fluid movement, Damien pulls me into his arms, holding me tight as I sob, all of my fear pouring out of me. I'm alive. I'm safe.

I'm with Damien.

For an eternity, we simply hold each other. Then he kisses me, long and deep, as if in proof that we're both still alive and safe and *us*.

An hour later, I stand in the doorway as the police and the ambulance leave. As it turns out, there had been reports over the last few years about Franklin's unusual behavior and his fascination with the serpent bracelet. Because of that, the police didn't question our story that he'd asked to buy it, and after we refused, he broke in and attacked me, destroying the bracelet in the process. No one other than Damien and I know what really happened, and already it's beginning to feel like a dream. Part of me is relieved. There are some memories that are better forgotten. But at the same time, part of me doesn't want to forget. It was our love that saved us, that kept us from truly becoming what Franklin had tried to make us.

Our love, I think, when Damien takes my hand. And for the billionth time I wonder how I ever got so lucky to have a man like Damien.

"This wasn't what I intended when I bought you Vivien Lorainne's house as a present," he says once the departing sirens have faded.

I laugh. "No? I wasn't sure. After all, you do like to make a splash, Mr. Stark."

He chuckles, but when he turns to me, his expression is serious. "We'll put it on the market today."

I draw a breath as I meet his eyes. Despite the chaos and destruction that surrounds us, I've never felt more loved. More lucky. More alive.

"No," I say. "We'll keep it."

"Keep it?"

I nod as I take both his hands, then squeeze them.

Even as I do, I feel the details of the last few days slipping away, and I somehow know that soon we will both have forgotten. Anything we might recall will seem like nothing more than a bad dream.

I'm glad of that. And yet....

I draw in a breath and shake my head. "It's a reminder of who we are," I tell him. "Of how strong we are. Even if we forget all of this tomorrow, the house will still be standing. Proof that together, we can survive anything."

I watch his face as the doubt slowly fades, replaced by that deliciously sexy smile.

"We're forever, you and I." His voice curls through me. "In this life, and in whatever comes after, you're mine."

"Yes," I whisper, my heart full to bursting. "For always."

THE END

ABOUT THE AUTHOR

J. Kenner (aka Julie Kenner) is the *New York Times, USA Today, Publishers Weekly, Wall Street Journal* and #1 International bestselling author of over one hundred novels, novellas and short stories in a variety of genres.

In her previous career as an attorney, JK worked as a lawyer in Southern California and Texas. She currently lives in Central Texas, with her husband, two daughters, and two rather spastic cats.

Stay in touch! Text JKenner to 21000 to subscribe to JK's text alerts.

www.jkenner.com